The War, Love, & Harmony Series: Book 4
The Sheik's Angry Bride

Elizabeth Lennox

Note: Books 1 and 2 in The War, Love, & Harmony Series are free e-books. Learn more about the series or download the free books at ElizabethLennox.com.

CONTENTS

About the War, Love, and Harmony Series   1

Chapter 1   5

Chapter 2   16

Chapter 3   25

Chapter 4   34

Chapter 5   40

Chapter 6   55

Chapter 7   59

Chapter 8   73

Chapter 9   78

Chapter 10   83

Chapter 11   88

Epilogue   95

Excerpt from The Sheik's Blackmailed Bride,
Book 5 in The War, Love, and Harmony Series   98

List of Elizabeth Lennox Books   110

About the War, Love, and Harmony Series

This series encompasses two generations of love stories across the four fictional neighboring countries of Larcatia, Altair, Lurasa, and Tularia. When the four betrothed princes and princesses fall in love with the wrong partner, a devastating chain of events is set into motion. Only the future leaders can put things right.

The first two stories tell the tales of two princes and their unplanned romances. These books are available free as e-books from ElizabethLennox.com.

Fighting with the Infuriating Prince: Jalayla couldn't believe the arrogance of the man! To actually order her around? How rude! But beneath the surface of her anger towards the handsome prince, there was a simmering heat, an uninvited fascination with the man that she couldn't seem to fight. Every time he touched her, every time he even looked at her, she felt that strange sensation.

Tasir wanted to fire her at first sight. She argued with him about everything and challenged him in ways that no other woman dared. So why did he want to pick the woman up and make love to her? Initially, he didn't know that the lovely woman with fiery eyes and a sensuous figure was the one and only Princess Jalayla. And was determined that he would have her for his own.

So what's a man to do when he finds out that the woman of his dreams is promised to marry another man?

Dancing with the Dangerous Prince: Jalayla couldn't believe the arrogance of the man! To actually order her around? How rude! But beneath the surface of her anger towards the handsome prince, there was a simmering heat, an uninvited fascination with the man that she couldn't seem to fight. Every time he touched her, every time he even looked at her, she felt that strange sensation.

Tasir wanted to fire her at first sight. She argued with him about everything and challenged him in ways that no other woman dared. So why did he want to pick the woman up and make love to her? Initially, he didn't know that the lovely woman with fiery eyes and a sensuous figure was the one and only Princess Jalayla. And was determined that he would have her for his own.

So what's a man to do when he finds out that the woman of his dreams is promised to marry another man?

Two weddings! Two love matches that weren't supposed to be! Princess Ciara of Altair, previously engaged to Prince Tasir went on to marry Prince Zoran of Larcatia. While Prince Tasir of Lurasa weds Princess Jalayla of Tularia.

Unfortunately, the weddings don't result in peace. The two couples were able to experience only a short-lived interlude of calm before tensions escalated to the point that violence was inevitable. Even after the weddings and despite years of trying to calm the problems, the four countries break out into war. A ten year, brutal war that was never supposed to be.

Sheik Zahir del Hassar Alzar of Larcatia brings the three other ruling sheiks to the Fortress of the Guards in secret. These four men – some recently risen to their power, others who have been rulers for a few years – all agree that it is time to stop the war caused by the tensions that were started when their parents or ancestors married years ago. The fighting has been going on too long and nothing has been gained. Borders remain as they were before the wars took place and the reasons for fighting don't seem to apply any longer. The broken marriage contracts never should have resulted in war; peace must be restored for the benefit of all four countries.

After long and challenging negotiations, the four rulers agree to cease hostilities and sign treaties so that the healing process can begin. They devise a strategy to help their people diffuse the rivalries and tensions that have developed. The four men agree that the best way to show their subjects that life should move on, without war, is to each marry and produce an heir. Royal weddings and the birth of a new generation will give the people a reason to hope.

The saga continues with another generation, where the now-current rulers of Larcatia, Altair, Lurasa, and Tularia must fulfill their treaty obligations.

The Sheik's Secret Bride: Their story began five years ago. Callie fell madly, crazily in love with Zahir. But the war in his country was raging and nurturing their relationship was tenuous at best. When Callie was captured, the experience was terrifying. Zahir found and rescued her, but he knew it would be impossible to insulate her from danger in his country. Despite his wishes to be together, he knew that to keep her safe he must send her away. However, he wouldn't let her go until she was his bride. In a secret wedding, he married her, and then spirited her to safety.

She arrived in her haven traumatized, fearful, homeless…and pregnant. Slowly, she rebuilt her life, gave birth to her son and somehow learned to get on with living without Zahir. For five long years, Callie recovered from the nightmare of her captivity. And she raises her son.

When Zahir enters her life once more, she can't believe that the fire between them is hotter than before. But she refuses to give in, despite its intensity. She's too afraid that the peace between the previously warring countries will end and that she or her son could be in peril again. She yearns to feel safe, but can she defy her heart or deny her son his father?

The Sheik's Angry Bride: Duty. Responsibility. Those were the priorities of Layla's upbringing. So when her father announced that she is to marry the Sheik of Lurasa, she accepted her duty and steeled her heart to a loveless life of obligation.

What she refused to accept was Garon's intense effect on her. The man wasn't what she anticipated! And he wouldn't conform to her plans or expectations. This was an arranged marriage! They had appearances to maintain, duties to adhere to. Why were these crazy feelings flying between them every time he touched her?

Garon entered into the marriage expecting only to be faithful to his wife and to the agreement he had made with the other sheiks. What he wasn't expecting was a fiery beauty that set his senses on fire or the intense need to have her. Responsibility be damned, this woman was his! And he was going to teach her about living and loving.

The Sheik's Blackmailed Bride: Luna couldn't believe the chain of events that had led to her wedding day. All she'd wanted was to save her small village, to help the residents to get out from underneath their crippling debt. So she'd written to the man who owned the bank. And here she was, walking down the aisle toward a man she barely knew. A man who could make her body sing but who could crush her hopes and dreams with a few harsh words.

Dassar needed a wife. The lovely Luna fit none of his criteria. She was too soft, too sweet and would be hurt by palace life. So why couldn't he forget her? Why could she get under his skin so easily? And why couldn't he simply walk away?

The Sheik's Convenient Bride: The only reason Kylie had come back to the palace was to prove to everyone that she was over Tarek. Her girlish infatuation was a thing of the past. So how did she end up dining with the sheik? And why was her body still vibrating when he kissed her? Why couldn't she simply put her infatuation in the past where it belonged?

Tarek took one look at the fascinating beauty and knew that Kylie was the woman he was going to have for his wife. He didn't want to marry, but the terms of the peace treaty were absolute. So if he had to do it, why not do it with the lovely, feisty and sexy woman that he couldn't get out of his mind?

Note to readers: Although the books of the series are related by this shared backstory, each is an independent story in its own right. With the preceding context for reference, the books may be read out of order. Books 1 and 2 are free e-books and may be downloaded from ElizabethLennox.com.

Chapter 1

Layla smoothed the long, black gloves up over her arms and elbows, ignoring the pains in her stomach. She would not give in to the nausea. This is what she had been trained for. This moment, this role…all her life she'd been told that this was her purpose. All of the details of the contract had been negotiated, each aspect of the agreement had been debated and finalized, every line of the contract had ultimately been signed by the appropriate people. Not by her, of course! No, she hadn't been called into any office to sign the agreement. But that didn't matter. This moment represented everything for which she'd been instructed and coached since birth.

She took a deep breath and focused all of her attention on ensuring that there were no wrinkles in her dress or her gloves, that the diamond bracelet on her wrist didn't show the clasp, and refused to contemplate what was about to happen. Her gloved hand reached up and smoothed her hair, then stopped. There was so much hairspray on her right now, the friction of touching it in any way might light her head on fire.

Layla might have smiled at the idea if she weren't so terrified inside. That didn't stop the image from forming though. She could just picture her fiancée's face when he walked into this meeting room only to discover a standing ball of flames instead of his fiancée. Of course, Layla would stand perfectly upright, a smile of greeting on her overly made up features as she bowed and tried not to let the flames from her hair touch any of the medals on her intended's immaculate and exalted chest. But that was what she'd been trained all of her life for – to look acceptable at every moment of the day and produce heirs. No other reason – just to adorn her husband's arm and act as a walking womb.

A burst of hysterical laughter threatened, but she took a deep breath and tried hard to remain composed despite her overly active imagination. It wouldn't do for her to be caught laughing when she met her future husband for the first time. Layla cringed inwardly because even her inner dialogue now sounded like her mother, admonishing her for being silly. Regardless, she pulled her shoulders back and took a deep breath, trying to snap out of the terror she was feeling. No, it definitely wouldn't do to appear to be smiling. And laughing? Out of the question, she told herself mentally. A pleasant expression was all that was needed during this meeting. Anything more might offend, anything less might insult.

Over and over, this had been drilled into her, to the point where she now could breathe in, breathe out, and then look up with the perfectly serene expression on her face that she'd been forced to practice while growing up.

She was also painfully aware that smiling too brightly might cause her makeup to crack. Goodness, wouldn't that be silly? She could see the headlines tomorrow morning… "A chunk of the princess' face fell to the floor after she laughed!"

No, she mentally shook herself. That wouldn't do, either. Serenity, she chanted to herself. She'd practiced this look in the mirror so often, it should come naturally to her by now. Breathe in. Breathe out. Lift the chin. Hands calm. Spine straight. And don't throw up on the man! For goodness sake, don't throw up!

The doors at the other end of the hallway opened up and she pulled her shoulders back. Showtime, she thought, and suppressed the resentment that was welling up inside of her.

She waited patiently, her light blue eyes glancing across each man's face as he stepped through the doors, wondering who would be her future husband. She was relieved to be wearing the high necked, black satin sheath dress, so that her pounding heart wouldn't be noticed. This was the night her hopes and dreams were to die. This was the night when all of her silly girl fantasies would be obliterated.

This was the night when she met her new owner.

Garon stepped through the double doors just as his guards separated to the right and left. His eyes moved through the crowd of people standing inside the room, taking them all in. But his gaze skidded to a screeching halt as he caught sight of the trembling beauty standing in the middle of the room. There was no way he could miss the fact that this was his bride-to-be. The other guests, including her mother and father, were all standing near the walls. This stunning beauty stood in the center, watching him with her lovely fairy eyes and soft, full lips; her slender figure was clad all in black from her neck right down to her long fingers and her dainty toes.

Two things occurred to him at that moment. The first was that his exquisite fiancée had come to their first meeting dressed for a funeral – which amused him. He had no doubt that the message was intended.

But the other thought was regarding her beauty, which was quite startling. He'd seen formal pictures of her, of course. The negotiations for this marriage had taken place over the past several months, so he knew well what Layla Alfarsi looked like. But he was startled by the impact of her, which was not something he had anticipated. He wanted to be attracted to his wife – that was a given. What he hadn't foreseen were his physical reactions to her. They hit him like a punch in the gut.

Another feeling – a primal and voracious anticipation that surged up inside of him as he approached his future bride – was also unanticipated. And he wasn't sure it was welcome either.

The entire reason for this meeting was to get to know his bride before the wedding. Not to toss her over his shoulder so he could carry her away to a private place and have his way with her.

Reigning in his near blinding need to possess this woman, he stopped directly in front of her. Looking down at her, he was surprised at how small she seemed. According to the dossier he'd been given on Layla Alfarsi, she was supposed to be five feet, five inches tall. But this woman, even in heels, barely came to his shoulder. Her slight form, her willowy figure, probably made her appear smaller, he thought.

"Good evening, Layla," he started off. He reached down and took her hand, irritated with the long gloves. He wanted to rip them off of her, to feel her soft skin and explore those pink lips. But she might get offended by that, he supposed.

All in due time, he reminded himself. Very soon, this woman would be his. And he could explore all of that trembling courage at his leisure.

"Good evening, Your Highness," she replied, dipping into a curtsy and bowing her head.

Layla couldn't believe how hard it was to rise from that simple gesture but her legs were trembling and her heart pounding so hard, she was actually worried that she might fall onto the floor at this man's feet. He must have sensed her trepidation because his hand tightened on her fingers, helping her to rise out of the curtsy. When she was once more standing in front of him, she knew that the polite thing to do was to thank him silently but she simply couldn't look up at him. Not this man!

He was too...everything! Shock waves rocketed throughout her body as the heat from his hand seemed to be melting the silk of her black gloves where he continued to touch her. She'd tried to pull her hand away, but he wouldn't release her fingers.

Layla felt trapped by this man. He was barely touching her, but there was something about him, a sense deep inside of her that told her she should run as fast and as hard as she could away from him.

But her training kicked in once more and she straightened her shoulders. Waiting.

And waiting. In fact, everyone in the room seemed to be silent, waiting.

"We will stand here all night, little one, until you look at me," he told her in a voice that only she could hear.

Layla's heart, already pounding fast, went into triple time with his words. Look at him? She wanted to run away! She wanted to hide behind the enormous plant in the corner. She wanted to whip her hand out from his grasp and step backwards so there was more space between the two of them. She absolutely did not want to look up at him.

But this was her duty. He'd commanded, she must obey. Gritting her teeth, she forced her eyes higher. And higher! Goodness, he was tall!

When her blue eyes finally met his, that horrible trembling increased even more. His black gaze looked down at her and that need to flee, to hide, intensified. But something else also rose up. Something that saved her from making a fool of herself and bringing dishonor upon her family.

Anger!

Oh, the wonderful, heat-encouraging, bubbling anger was her saving grace. Gritting her teeth, she stared right back at this man, daring him to…to do whatever it was he might do! She had no idea of his intentions, nor was she going to ask. She simply waited for him, challenging him with her blue eyes as they fought a battle of wills.

Garon's stomach muscles clenched and his body reacted to that angry gaze. Until a few months ago, he'd never really contemplated his wife and the traits he might want in that woman. Nor had there been any discussion during the negotiations about Layla's preferences, her temperament. He was simply assured that she had been raised to know her duty, her responsibilities. Testing had been done to ensure her fertility and that was the end of that conversation. All the negotiations from that point on were monetary and political. The exchange of this woman from her family to his would be a boon to both sides of the negotiating table.

Every feral and predatory cell in his body reacted to her challenge, to those striking, blue eyes glaring up at him. He wanted to both subdue her rebellion while at the same time, set her passion free. The unexpected pleasure he found in just looking at her shot through him and he had to stop himself from ordering everyone out of the room but this one woman.

"You are more beautiful than I expected," he finally said, breaking the charged silence between them. He didn't give a damn about the others in the room. In fact, he wondered why his staff had arranged for this first meeting to take place in front of so many people. It should have been private.

So instead of saying all the things he wanted to say, or touch her to see if her skin was as soft as it looked, he restrained himself. He wanted to make this woman more comfortable so he pulled back and dug deep for all of those gentlemanly lessons his mother had tried very hard to instill within him.

"You will be a beautiful asset to my country," he said, bowing over her hand.

Garon almost laughed when his fairy-eyed beauty almost rolled her eyes at his comment.

"Thank you, Your Highness," she replied with a polite, if slightly bored, tone of voice.

He smothered his amusement as he realized that his lovely, soon-to-be bride wasn't so shallow that a compliment could sway her. "Come. We will dine and you will tell me about yourself," he stated, tucking her hand onto his arm and leading her towards yet another set of double doors.

Layla didn't argue with him. Nor did she counter his command with the comment that he might want to tell her about himself as well. Instead, she fell back on her training, using all of her energy to force polite conversation through her stiff lips. "You have a beautiful country," she said, starting in with all of her well-rehearsed platitudes. Her mother had given her a list, a script almost, of things for Layla to discuss during this initial meeting. The beauty of his country was the first and foremost, even though she'd flown into the country early this morning and had been chauffeured in a limousine with dark windows right to the palace. The most she could state with any personal knowledge was that the sunrise was striking at dawn.

She grumbled resentfully at that reminder as she walked beside the man, wondering if he knew what time she'd been woken this morning. The sun hadn't even been coming up over the horizon when her maid had knocked on her door. Her mother followed closely behind to supervise Layla's final preparations before boarding the plane that would take them here. He had probably been lolling in bed with his latest mistress while she'd been poked and prodded, her nails re-manicured, her toes re-pedicured, her eyebrows plucked, her skin scrubbed, her dark hair brushed and numerous chemicals applied so that it would 'glow'. That only brought to mind her earlier thought about her hair catching on fire and she actually pulled back when they walked through the doors as she noticed all the candles that were decorating the tables. She almost laughed, but she compressed her lips and fought to regain control of her amusement.

"Something has amused you," he observed and she was surprised that he was so astute. She glanced up at him, then darted her gaze away, unable to maintain eye contact with that intense, black look.

"Tell me," he commanded as he allowed a servant to pull out her chair. His hand tightened its hold on her fingers when she was about to sit, silently telling her that he wanted an answer before she sat down.

"I was simply delighted with the ambiance, Your Highness," she lied and raised her eyes up to his once more, daring him to call out her lie. She had no idea that her lips were tilted up or that her crystal blue eyes were looking at him with the most outrageous defiance.

He looked down at her and couldn't suppress the chuckle. "You're a beautiful liar," he told her but bowed as she delicately lowered herself onto the chair.

Layla blushed, not used to being called out so arrogantly and openly. In her world and from her experience, one simply didn't express one's thoughts. What was he thinking?!

"You are very charming, Your Highness," she replied and lowered her lashes so that he couldn't see what she was thinking about that whopper. But when he simply chuckled once again, the pink stain to her cheeks turned an even brighter color. Instead of looking at him again, which she wasn't sure she could do anyway, she turned to face the others who were all filing in according to rank.

It took bare moments before all were seated, none wanting to make their ruler wait for his dinner. After a curt nod, the servants filed in with the first course, placing the cold cucumber and avocado soup in front of each person.

Layla swallowed and turned her head quickly away, not wanting to smell the cucumbers. Why anyone would ruin an avocado by pairing it with a cold cucumber soup was beyond her comprehension. But she carefully picked up her spoon and tasted the soup, willing herself not to gag. It was close, but she finally swallowed the spoonful and even went back for more.

She heard the chuckle beside her on her third spoonful.

"I apologize, Your Highness," she said, laying her spoon down and turning to face her soon-to-be husband. "I missed whatever was funny."

Garon wanted to laugh again, but he refrained. "You know, if you don't like the soup, you don't have to eat it."

Layla blinked, surprised that he'd noticed. "The soup is extremely well prepared, Your Highness." But she didn't lift her spoon again, using their conversation as the reason to not sample more of the vile concoction.

He shook his head. "A very cautious and subtle answer. I'm impressed," he replied back. His eyes mirrored his admiration. "You obviously hate the soup and yet you came up with a perfectly acceptable response that wasn't a lie. Very diplomatically stated."

Layla's stomach clenched with the realization that this man, her future husband, was so perceptive. And outspoken!

She searched her brain quickly, trying to come up with some way to cover her obvious flub. "Nonsense, Your Highness. I'm merely enjoying the meal and the company." She looked out over the rest of the group. All of them were pretending to converse with each other, but she could feel their curiosity. Each and every one of them was straining to hear what the two of them were talking about. Thankfully, Garon was aware of their interest and was carefully keeping their conversation low so that it was just between the two of them.

She was grateful, but that didn't help her in the long term. She would still have to marry this man – still have to go through the rest of her life under his dictates. Her whole life would be catering to his likes and dislikes…and eating disgusting, revolting cucumber soup.

He noticed the set look in her eyes and the way her jaw was clenched tightly closed. Not to mention her stiff shoulders and the flash in her eyes – all signs that told him that she was in a fighting mood, but trying hard to remain polite. "You say you like Lurasa," he opened with that conversation. "What do you like the best? What have you seen so far?"

Layla's stomach clenched with this new question. Fortunately, her mother had prepared her extremely well. There had been an entire folder of information Layla had memorized, including the history, culture and politics. "Well…" and she listed off some of the famous sites that she'd seen in the file that had included pictures and comments from others who had visited before. When she was finished, her shoulders sagged with relief that her memory hadn't yet failed her.

Garon wasn't sure what was wrong with what she'd said, but he knew that there was a great deal more to the issue. She was hiding something.

It had been a simple question, he thought. The weather and tourist attractions were always a safe subject and he'd employed those topics numerous times in the past to help a person relax so they might open up a bit more. So what was wrong with the way she'd described so many of the attractions? He couldn't quite put his finger on the problem, but he knew there was one.

"And when did you see the moon gardens?" he asked, watching her lovely features, knowing he'd just trapped her. The moon gardens were a huge attraction, especially on the weekends. Tourists and locals alike walked through a lush garden filled with white flowers, some of which only came out at night, and all the white reflected the moon's light, making the area look as if it was perhaps invaded by exotic night creatures. It was enchanting and he'd walked through the gardens on several occasions when he was younger. Not lately though. Now that the war was over, visitors were flocking to the interesting sites, including the moon gardens. It was almost impossible and unfair to close down the garden to tourists just so that he could have a bit of relaxation.

He also had a hard time seeing this elegant, reserved woman sweating it up the steep mountain, nor could he imagine her traipsing through the dirt pathways in her very delicate shoes. It wasn't an easy trek up and some of the pathways clung onto the edge of a cliff and could be a bit intimidating for the faint of heart.

Layla glanced nervously at the man. "I saw them just the other day," she told him honestly, not mentioning that it had been via a picture. She hadn't actually visited the site. But she was game for battle. Instead of arguing with him, she turned it around. "What is your favorite site?" she asked.

"Oh, I think that moon gardens has to rank on up there as one of the top sites." He watched her eyes as they narrowed ever so slightly. "Did you do the banana trip down?" he asked, not laughing in any way.

"I don't think so," she told him. "There's no banana trip. In fact," she sat up straighter and turned more fully to face him, "I've never heard of any sort of banana trip. Please tell me more."

Garon had to give it to her. She wasn't backing down or admitting anything. "Which way did you walk up?" One could walk down the mountain, which was still a difficult hike. Or for the truly adventurous, a person could zip line down from the top, all the way to the bottom in the darkness. It was terrifying if one didn't watch carefully for the signals on when to slow down with the heavy leather gloves provided, but it was still an interesting way to challenge one's self.

Layla was stumped with that question but she rallied. "I only know of the one way to go up and down which is via the pathway."

"Impressive stairs, wouldn't you say?"

She had absolutely no clue what he meant. She'd read that the climb was just a rough pathway and nowhere did the information she read had there been mention of any stairs. "Stairs tend to be washed away by the elements."

He sipped his wine, lifting a dark eyebrow. "Why don't you just admit that you've never been to see the gardens?" he asked, daring her to be brave enough.

Layla shifted in her chair angrily. This man had just kept giving her more and more rope to hang herself so she wasn't giving in. "One doesn't have to actually experience something to appreciate it. You only asked me which of the attractions I liked."

He thought back to the beginning of the conversation and she was right. "Touché, my beauty."

"And in that same light, do you really think that the woman you are about to marry to would be allowed to do something as inelegant as traipsing up a mountain and walking through gardens at night?" she asked, taking her glass of wine and looking out at the other guests.

Garon looked at her closely and something about the way she carefully set her glass down on the table told him loudly that she resented that restriction.

"So you would have wanted to experience the gardens and not just read about them, is that it?"

She shook her head. "Don't be ridiculous," she snapped and then realized what she'd just said. Looking up at him, she opened her mouth to apologize.

Garon stopped her with a wave of his hand. "Don't you dare apologize, Layla," he told her in a soft voice that only she could hear. "I want you to be free to say anything you want to me."

Her eyes widened with that announcement, but looking at him, she didn't believe him. "Yes, well, thank you for that," she said with as much graciousness as she could muster. "I still should apologize for my tone. It was inexcusable."

Garon considered the lovely woman who had latent fire underneath that cool exterior. He wanted to release that fire, wanted to experience her passion – in all forms. He wasn't exactly sure how to do that though.

"What sorts of things would you want to experience that you've been denied so far?" he asked.

Layla placed her hands carefully on her lap while the wait staff cleared out the soup and placed a salad in front of her. "I'm sure that whatever opportunities that you have in mind for the future will be quite stimulating," she replied with as much diplomacy as she could muster under the circumstances. She then picked up her fork and stabbed an innocent piece of lettuce.

"But if you were in charge, what would the Queen of Lurasa do?"

"I'm not in charge," she replied, unaware of how her fairy blue eyes burned with unspoken words. "So perhaps you could tell me how you picture my role."

Garon shook his head, fascinated by the delicate way she was flicking each of the carefully laid out lettuce leaves and vegetables. Oh, she was more than angry, he thought with fascination. "I didn't ask you what you thought I might want. I asked you to tell me what you wanted, how you pictured your role or would want it if you were in charge."

She turned and glared at him. "I am not in charge, Your Highness. Perhaps if I were…"

"Let's just pretend, shall we?"

She sighed and almost dropped her fork. But she regained her patience at the last moment before she let loose on him. "Let us not live in a fantasy world, Your Highness. It would be so much more kind if we stuck to reality and left the authors and painters to live in a fantasy world."

"So you're not even going to venture into the realm of possibilities?"

She put her fork carefully beside her plate, once again laying her hands on her lap. It was a trick she'd learned early on to control a potential outburst that dared to bubble up from the depths of her temper. The act of folding her hands onto her lap gave her mind something to focus on besides whatever it was that was irritating her.

Never had she been this challenged though. It was almost as if her future husband was trying to get her to lose her temper, but why would he do that?

For the next forty minutes and throughout the numerous courses that were served by the ever-efficient palace staff, he challenged her docility more than any other person ever had, more than she'd thought was possible! Every calm, tedious topic she could think of, he would find a way to press her buttons. Was he mocking her? Even topics as non-provocative as the weather were tempting her to toss her ice water over his head.

When she realized what she'd just done, that she'd been arguing with her future husband, with the Sheik of Lurasa, she gasped, her eyes widened and she looked up at his eyes.

But she didn't see condemnation there!

Was that…admiration?

Layla was confused and she ducked her head down, trying to quiet her racing nerves. His expression startled her and she didn't understand her reaction to him. All she knew was that she'd acted outside of her prescribed role and he hadn't smacked her back into place. There was silence in the room, indicating that the others had also heard the two of them arguing and weren't sure what to think.

Layla shivered with fear. She couldn't believe she'd so carelessly disregarded the lessons of decorum and palace protocol that had been drilled into her from early childhood. She'd been raised to this role. She knew the parameters around which women were allowed to act and speak. How could she so completely have ignored those rules?

"I apologize, Your Highness," she whispered fervently, her head still bowed. She could feel her parents' censorious eyes upon her but couldn't look up.

"You're apologizing for what?" he demanded. "For having an opinion? I consider that a very attractive aspect of your personality. Please don't stop," he said very softly but with just as much intensity as her apology had been delivered. He took her hand. "We will have dessert and coffee in a more relaxed atmosphere," he declared. "I'd like to hear more about your opinions on the issues you brought up." With that, he gently tugged her hand and lifted her out of the chair, feeling her reluctance to follow him. He understood, but there was no way he was letting her back down. She was fascinating and passionate and he had seen the fire inside of her.

Two hours ago, he hadn't thought he'd wanted an opinionated wife, hadn't even contemplated the personality of his wife. All he'd wanted was a woman at the appropriate child bearing age who knew how to act and react in a diplomatic manner. Her appearance had been important, he had to produce a child with the woman, but they had been secondary to her manners. But after the last hour, he knew that he wouldn't have Layla any other way. He wanted all of that passion and excitement. As she'd argued with him, he'd discovered that she was intelligent and insightful, had brought up some interesting ideas that hadn't previously been considered and he was impressed. Suddenly, it was imperative that he hear more, to discuss other topics. The idea of an insipid wife who didn't bother with anything more than fashions or makeup and shoes, was not what he wanted now.

He wanted Layla.

Chapter 2

Layla paced back and forth in the enormous office, her anger simmering the longer she waited.

He'd demanded this meeting, she thought with resentment. Why had he arrogantly commanded her presence and then not even bothered to show up? He'd "requested" her presence thirty minutes ago according to the summons she'd received through a servant. Since this meeting had not been on the official schedule, she'd frantically had to shift the day's priorities. This meant she was no longer meeting with the wedding coordinator then the designers. The appointments she'd had with potential candidates for positions on the staff would have to be rearranged despite the fact that several of those interviewees were already on route to the palace. Instead, she had raced to shower and change her clothes, hurrying to the man's office, almost breathless so that she could arrive on time, only to be told that he was called away for "a moment" and would be with her soon.

She'd been slightly miffed by that announcement when she'd arrived. But now she'd had, glancing at her watch again, thirty-five minutes to work up a righteous anger. How rude! How obnoxious! The man was completely insensitive to other's schedules!

She refused to admit that a large portion of her anger was simple nervousness at seeing the man again. Last night, he'd caused her to step outside of the role she'd been assigned to play and she didn't like that he had that kind of power over her. She hated that she'd deviated from the script. She'd given herself a long lecture after the dinner and she'd been back on track this morning, but here she was, once more becoming angry instead of finding that serene place inside of her that could protect her from…well, all that was going to happen. This marriage…she shook her head, trying to think instead of react.

She looked at his office, eyeing the big, leather chair that appeared to be extra comfortable. Defiantly, she walked around the desk, letting her hand smooth along the leather, unconcerned that she should be on the other side of the man's desk, waiting patiently for his glorious presence to arrive.

The obviously well-used chair wasn't new, but it had aged beautifully over the years. His body had polished the leather to a sheen and, as she dared to sit down in the enormous chair, she wondered what it would be like to have this kind of power. It would be nice to have people grovel at her feet instead of her trying to anticipate and avoid any sort of insult to the rest of the world.

Her hands smoothed against the leather, contemplating all of the things she would demand. She pulled a pad of paper closer, looking at the notes there. Since they were some stupid calculations, formulas that she had no idea what they meant, she flipped the paper over to a clean sheet. Grabbing his pen, she leaned back in the chair, propping her elegant shoes up on the edge of his desk, just as she'd seen her father do on numerous occasions while some poor soul trembled in front of his desk, taking orders and trying desperately to anticipate her father's requirements.

She tapped the pen against her chin, contemplating what orders she would give to Garon if their roles were reversed. First, she'd stop this wedding. Yep, that would definitely be at the top of her list. She looked out the window, then smiled, eagerly writing down the next item she would decree. All men would be forced into charm school. As a sub item under that one, she wrote "show women equal respect" and "no arranged marriages".

She had added several more items to her list and was really getting into the task, forgetting that she was here in this office to meet with her future husband. "You look too happy to be doing anything good," a deep voice said too close to her shoulder.

Gone was all of her poise and diplomatic reserve. Layla sprung out of the chair with a gasp of horror, astonished that she'd been caught doing anything so irreverent as to be sitting in the man's chair.

"I'm so sorry!" she breathed, trying to back up.

Once again, Garon felt captivated by this woman. He had enjoyed a spirited conversation with her the previous evening but as soon as she remembered others were around, she'd retreated behind her shell of civility. Dessert and coffee in the anteroom were a tedious and boring hour during which he tried to pull her back out of that unexciting, reserved shell that she hid behind, but he'd been unsuccessful.

Instead of letting her move away this time, he trapped her. His body easily shifting so that she was caught between him and his desk. Her sexy, round bottom had been sitting in his chair. He couldn't let her disrespect go unpunished, he told himself with a secret smile.

"What were you doing sitting at my desk?" he asked.

Layla tried to move to his right, but his extremely large body stopped that escape route. When she tried to slip away from him to the left, he blocked that getaway just as effectively. Trapped, she bowed her head, hoping he would just let this slip go.

"I'm sorry. It was inappropriate of me to invade your desk area," she whispered even as she resentfully thought that it was just a stupid chair, not to mention, he'd left her cooling her heels for almost an hour.

"You were making a list?" he asked and she gasped when he bent over, causing her to bend backwards in order to avoid her breasts touching his muscular chest. She was so focused on avoiding any contact with him that she almost forgot what she'd written on that pad of paper. "That's nothing!" she said and tried to grab it out of his hands.

But Garon only lifted the notepad higher, out of her reach but he "helped" her by wrapping his strong arm around her waist, bringing her right where he wanted her to be, against his chest.

"What does this list mean?" he asked, amusement lacing his words as his eyes read the title. "If I were in charge…" he read out loud.

Looking down into her almost glowing blue eyes, a black eyebrow went up in question. "So the little fairy has a bit of a sting to her? Want to rule the world, little one?" he asked.

"No," she replied honestly. She just wanted to be able to rule herself, she thought, still trying to get out of his arms. The steel band around her waist was more unsettling than she wanted to admit. "Let me go," she whispered, wishing she sounded more stern and less breathless. And she wished that her body hadn't started trembling at the first sound of his voice because it was just getting worse, the longer she stood in his arms.

Garon looked down at her, noticed the points of her breasts that were pressed against his chest. "I don't think I'm going to do that," he told her with a husky voice.

"We shouldn't be touching like this."

"Why not? You're going to be my wife very soon."

"Yes but…"

"And I like touching you. You're very soft. Very responsive," he murmured.

She didn't like him thinking along those lines. "I'm not at all," she argued.

"So why is your heart racing," he asked, his thumb tracing the delicate bones under her neck. "And why do you tremble in my arms?"

Her chin went up a notch and she wasn't sure if she was trying to stop him from touching her or defy him. "I'm afraid of you," she told him.

He thought about that for a moment. "You shouldn't be," he countered. "But tell me why I make you nervous."

She glared up at him, pretending she wasn't shivering like a rag doll. "I'm not nervous. I'm afraid of you. There's a significant difference."

He chuckled, enjoying the way she was still trying to get out of his embrace. "Explain the difference to me," he commanded.

Layla felt his hard muscles of his thighs against her, very aware of how inappropriate their embrace really was. "This isn't right," she said and tried to push his hands away from her.

In order to stop him, she tried to step around him once more but he countered that move more effectively than she could have anticipated by simply slipping his leg between hers as soon as she moved.

Layla was so overwhelmed by this new sensation that she wasn't sure what to do. She simply stood there, his hard, muscular thigh pressing up against her feminine heat, her body throbbing embarrassingly in places she didn't want to admit were affected by him.

Garon saw her blush and couldn't have stopped his own body's reaction to her even if he'd wanted to – which he didn't. He was thrilled that his future wife was so responsive and pushed it even more by bending lower, his lips brushing ever so softly against the shell of her ear. "You feel wonderful in my arms, little one. I can't wait until our wedding night when we can experience more together."

Layla was breathing hard, unaware of her fingers gripping the man's rock hard biceps as she closed her eyes, trying to pretend that nothing was going on. "I think..." she stopped talking when his leg shifted ever so slightly.

"If you are able to think, then I'm not doing something right," he growled, the sound sending vibrations low in her belly.

"Your..."

"Don't you dare call me anything but Garon when I'm holding you like this," and he bit her ear lobe then soothed the nipped flesh.

"I can't..."

"You can," he argued right back before she could spout some nonsense his body didn't want to hear. "Let yourself go," he coaxed. "Feel what we can do to each other. It will make being married so much better."

Those words should have stopped her cold but he moved his hand downward, covering her bottom and she shivered in reaction.

If it weren't for the phone ringing at that point, Layla wasn't sure what might have happened. As it was, she didn't even hear the jarring sound. All she noticed was that Garon wasn't touching her in the same way and he sighed with obvious annoyance at the interruption, blowing the wisps of hair off of her forehead. "The trials of being needed," he grumbled, still holding her close while he reached behind her and lifted the phone, snapping at whoever had dared to interrupt.

Fortunately, whoever was on the line had some information that was important to Garon and his hold around her waist loosened just enough so that she was able to step away from him. She skittered around the desk, urgently needing to find space that was out of his arm's reach. He watched her, giving her a look that told her he knew exactly what she was doing. She shivered with both awareness and fear because the look in his eyes told her that he wasn't going to let her get away with her evasion.

Layla wasn't going to wait around to find out what he might do though. As soon as his eyes dropped, looking for something on his desk, she hurried towards the door. She had her hand on the knob, a breath away from escape when she heard his voice stop her. "Layla, don't you dare go through that door," he warned.

Layla turned around, her hand still holding the knob and freedom, as she looked back at him. Thankfully, he had a very large office so, in her mind, she had a running head start. "I have things I have to do," she told him, then spun around and pulled the door wide open, rushing through it before he could bark at her to stop.

She hurried down the long hallway until she found a place where she was alone. Leaning against the wall, she let her head fall back against the ornate tiles, closing her eyes as she tried desperately to pull herself back together. They had been together twice now and both times, she'd found herself feeling out of control. Last night during the argument and today in his arms, and neither instance was good.

Layla hated this! She refused to be attracted to Garon! He'd bought her! Money had been exchanged! Political favors traded! And no one had consulted her in any way! Neither her mother nor her father had come to her and asked if she would like to be married to the Sheik of Lurasa! The first she'd heard about her sale was when her father announced that the papers had been signed over dinner one night.

Layla knew that she was simply a commodity to both her father and Garon so she was not going to make his life any easier by giving in to his sexual demands. No, she would be cool and sophisticated. She would do her job as his wife just as he would do his as ruler of his people. And they would both move in their separate spheres. When the time came to produce an heir, she would submit to him, but there was absolutely no need to fall into his arms every time he curled his little finger!

And surely there was a way to procreate without all that messy…sex…stuff! The sheik had a very competent physician on staff in the palace. Couldn't they just do the deed in some sort of petri dish? She didn't like messes and she definitely didn't like the way she felt when the Sheik of Lurasa came close to her. She didn't want to even think about how out of control she felt when he touched her or kissed her! Goodness, just remembering caused her breathing to start to become erratic again.

No, it was better if their children were produced in a more sterile environment. Garon could do all of those…crazy, uninhibited things…to his mistress!

And if the thought of Garon touching another woman made her stomach feel as if it was going to throw up, well, she could just ignore that nausea as she ignored all the other little things about her life that she didn't like or agree with.

Feeling better, although not really sure how she was going to follow through on all of her goals, she straightened up, took a deep breath and started walking down the hallway once again. Where she was going, she had no idea since she was still too flustered to remember the agenda for the day.

And then it occurred to her that Garon had interrupted that agenda because he'd wanted to talk to her. Goodness, they'd certainly gotten off track, she thought.

Shaking her head as if she could easily ignore the past hour, she walked towards the rooms she'd been assigned to during the pre-wedding festivities. What she needed was a good, long run to get rid of all of this tension created by the wedding arrangements.

Not that she'd actually had to do anything, she thought as she pulled on a pair of stretchy shorts and a sports bra. She added a looser outer shirt and her running shoes before heading out to the gym.

Garon finally got off of the phone and his first thought was to get that woman back into his office. And back into his arms. They'd started something and he was determined to finish it! Damn her, she'd slipped out of here with fear in those fairy eyes and he didn't like that. He didn't want her to fear this chemistry they had together. It was mutual and she damn well had to know that.

He looked down at his papers, cursing all of his responsibilities and more determined than ever to get things cleared up enough so that he could take that woman on a proper honeymoon. He was going to explore his little fairy's body more thoroughly than even she could imagine. By the end of their time together, she wouldn't be running away from him ever again.

His eyes caught on the notepad she'd discarded and a faint smile formed on his hard mouth as he read the words. "If I were in charge..." So his fairy woman wants control, eh? He chuckled as he read through the list. Cancel the wedding? That wasn't going to happen. His eyebrow shot up at the next one. Charm school? She didn't think he was charming?

He could be charming. He thought of all the charming ways he could touch her, watch her catch on fire like she had a few moments ago in his arms. Yes, he could be extremely charming when he put his mind to it.

He frowned with the third item. She didn't think he respected her? He looked up, contemplating that comment. He respected her. He probably hadn't shown her but the very fact that he had listened to her arguments last night proved that he respected her.

Garon's mind sifted through their conversation and his body reacted again. He almost groaned at how badly he wanted to hunt down his beautiful fairy woman and make love to her. He loved the way she got all bristly when he was around but the moment he touched her, she melted in his arms. She was all woman, soft and passionate, making those sexy sounds that made his body ache.

Damn! His body was rock hard again for her and he had a meeting! He needed to speed this wedding along. He wasn't going to make it at this rate.

He walked into his meeting but his focus was still on his fairy woman. And all of the interesting ways he could touch her so that she could repeat some of those sounds she'd made in his office a while ago.

Layla pressed the speed button again on the treadmill. And again. Pushing herself harder and harder in an effort to find that running nirvana which had always helped her get through the stressful times of her life. The pounding of her feet, the rhythm of the run, music in her ears and nothing on her mind had always worked in the past. But it wasn't coming. Not this time. That man had ruined her run!

"Layla!" the voice broke through the music blasting in her ears and she almost tripped on the treadmill before she caught herself and balanced on the side rails.

"What's wrong, Mother?" she asked, fighting for patience. Her mother was a perfect example of why arranged marriages should be banned. Her parents barely endured each other and her mother sniped at him over the petty things, just to poke her father's temper. Layla had two older brothers, both of whom had married well and both worked in the political world. In her mother's eyes, her only failing was Layla. Despite her best efforts, her mother hadn't been able to train out the irritating independent streak that ran through her daughter's blood.

"You need to get ready!" and she tapped her wrist where her gold watch rested.

Layla rubbed her face with the towel. "It is only ten o'clock in the morning," she replied, wondering what sorts of torture were waiting for her at her mother's direction.

"You have lunch with His Highness in two hours, Layla!"

Layla's entire body stiffened with surprise. "That wasn't on the schedule!"

"His Highness put it on the schedule a half hour ago. If you had been paying attention to your messages, you would know this already. Now get down off of that contraption and get into the shower! There is very little time now to make you presentable!"

Layla almost groaned out loud. Two hours! She had two hours before she was due to arrive at the impromptu lunch!

"Mother, I don't think I need a new manicure and pedicure, just to have lunch with the man."

"Don't you dare speak so disrespectfully about your future husband, Layla," she admonished as she nudged her daughter towards the suite of rooms they'd been assigned for the wedding celebrations. But she pulled her hand back with disgust when she touched her daughter's sweaty back. "I don't know why you have to exercise," she sniffed. "It is such a waste of time, not to mention dirty."

Layla didn't mention the cardiovascular, mental and physical benefits of exercise. She'd heard this comment from her mother on several occasions. It was one area of Layla's life that she had control over so she exercised when she could, even waking up early in order to get an hour in the gym if she had a busy schedule.

Not that she would be allowed to work. Oh no! The horror of a woman actually wanting a job, a career and personal satisfaction was a complete anathema to her family – and most likely to Sheik Garon, Wanna-Be-King-of-Everything. Yes, that argument had been offered when Layla was younger. Her mother had drilled early on that a woman's "career" was to make her husband happy, his career was her priority. A woman entertained, looked beautiful, made her husband's home run smoothly and produced children. And she did all of this in a politically beneficial marriage. Politically beneficial for Layla's family…or more specifically, her father.

Of course, Layla's mother was reveling in this wedding as well. Layla's marriage to such a powerful sheik would raise her mother's standing in her circle of superficial acquaintances that masquerade around town as friends. Her mother was reveling in her newfound power as the future mother-in-law to a sheik.

Could Layla blame her mother for finding joy anywhere she could? She probably shouldn't, but Layla didn't want to follow in her footsteps. She wanted a life for herself, accomplishments that she was able to state clearly as her own and not simply those of her husband.

She sighed and followed behind her mother. She showered, dressed in a green sheath dress, slipped her feet into the matching green shoes then sat down so that the manicurist could redo her nails while the stylist worked on her hair. It took an hour and a half of primping and prepping before she was deemed "presentable".

And just like earlier this morning, she stood in the dining room for twenty minutes, not daring to sit down because she'd been trained that one did not sit until the ruler sat. She also had been warned not to ruin the lines of her dress by sitting down. She was supposed to "wow" her future husband with her figure, so carefully outlined with the sheath dress. So here she stood, pretending to be calm and collected when inside, she was alternately shivering with fear because of her morning incident in his office and raging with anger that he was making her wait yet again with no news about the time he might arrive.

The man had no manners!

"I'm sorry, ma'am," a servant came into the room, bowing. "His Highness has expressed regret that he has had to cancel your lunch meeting."

Layla stood there silently after the man delivered the message. She didn't move, she didn't smile, she barely even acknowledged the message in any way. She counted to ten before she moved even a muscle other than blinking. She counted yet again before she allowed herself to speak. "Thank you very much for that information. Please convey to His Highness my highest regards and regret that we were not able to share lunch at this time but I am at his service for any other appointments he would like to set up."

With that, she spun around on her heel and walked out of the dining room. She hadn't had breakfast and, three minutes ago, she was furious because her stomach was growling with hunger. But she wasn't hungry any longer. She was too angry to be hungry. With stiff shoulders, she walked back to her suite and carefully slipped out of the green dress.

Pulling on yet another exercise outfit, she mercilessly tied her shoes and headed right back to the gym. She probably looked ridiculous with her hair so perfectly coiffed and sprayed, but she didn't care. She knew that she wouldn't even need to pull her hair into a band to keep it off of her neck because there was so much hairspray in her hair right now, it wouldn't dare move!

Chapter 3

Layla sat in her chair under the shade awning, her back stiffly erect and her eyes as open as she could make them in the sunshine. Everyone else was wearing sunglasses to shade their eyes but this competition was to showcase her and Garon for the press and for his people. They wanted to see her and so sunglasses were not allowed.

Of course, Garon was wearing them, she thought with resentment.

She kept her hands politely in her lap, clapping graciously as each of the contestants stepped up to the various competitions. There were sword fighting, horse races and even camel races! Later this afternoon, shooting and archery were on the schedule. Even the midday meal would be an event that would include long tables filled with various delicacies. She and Garon would be sampling several of them for lunch.

She knew her role and she smiled, turned her head, applauded and laughed, ignoring the way her cheeks hurt. Her eyes felt as if they were on fire and she was wearing a special undergarment that would absorb any sweat that dared to come off of her body in the hundred and ten degree heat.

"You don't like the competitions?" Garon commented as he leaned closer to her.

Layla turned her head and smiled at him, clapping as one more competitor bowed out of the sword fighting competition.

"They are all very exciting," she replied as she tried to ignore the trickle of sweat that slid down the back of her neck.

"You look bored out of your mind." He watched her and caught the way her eyes opened ever so slightly.

"Not at all," she replied and she honestly wasn't bored. She found sword fighting very exciting. It was always amazing that two men could come out of such events with cuts and wounds and still smile as if they'd just had a great time.

"You're lying."

She shook her head. "Not at all," she countered. "It is just a little warm," she told him. The undergarment might keep her outer clothes sweat free, but the stupid contraption was hot! And tight!

"Let's go get some food," he told her, taking her hand and leading her out of the shaded area reserved for the two of them and the other high ranking officials within his cabinet. "And something cold to drink. I hate these times when I have to sit here in a suit in this kind of weather."

Layla couldn't stop the snort of shock at his comment. When he looked back down at her, she laughed. "You don't look like you're uncomfortable, Your Highness."

He shook his head. "You look like you'd like to take a sword to whoever thought up the idea of these competitions to celebrate our wedding."

Again, she couldn't stop the laughter. "Perhaps you are more perceptive than I gave you credit for," she replied back.

He handed her a glass filled with ice and water. "Ah, you think I don't see through your polite façade, my lady. But I can assure you, I see a great deal."

Her breath caught in her throat with his words and she wanted to dump the ice water down the inside of her dress as the blush stole up her neck.

His hand brushed against her back and she stiffened, shocked by his touch yet again. She almost choked on the water this time when she tried to drink it so instead, she simply set it down and moved on. "Shall we sample some of the foods?" she suggested, taking a step away from him and those hands that seemed to be touching her whenever possible.

But he followed her, his longer legs easily able to keep pace with her. They tried chicken and beef kabobs, cheese hand pies that were freshly baked and melted in her mouth. She was exclaiming about each of the dishes, truly amazed at the wonderful tastes of each flavorful dish when Garon tapped her shoulder. When she turned around, he was standing close, too close as always, but the real problem was that he was holding a piece of baklava for her.

Her eyes dropped from his to the fingers where he was holding the treat, her breath halted in her throat as she watched him, not sure what she should do or say.

All the chaos of the festivities, the reporters, various vendors and even her parents, faded away as she looked at his strong fingers and the morsel dripping with honey. Layla was both fascinated and horrified, her mind unable to function as she stared at his fingers. Every cell in her body reacted, her muscles clenched and her legs trembled. Garon moved closer. "Try it, Layla," he commanded.

Her eyes glanced up into his, her breath hitched and she felt as if she could to melt into a puddle at his feet, which had absolutely nothing to do with the heat from the sun and everything to do with the heat coming from his body.

"I can take…"

His fingers moved closer and she couldn't help but take the taste from his fingers. As the honey and his taste hit her tongue, she moaned softly. Her lips curled around his fingers and she suddenly didn't want him to take them away. She wanted more, she wanted to suck his finger into his mouth and taste more of him.

"Excellent," he said, his voice deeper. Huskier.

She forgot to breathe for a long moment. When she heard his voice, her eyes popped open and she looked up at him, her world and all concepts about what was right and good and appropriate were banished with the touch of his finger when he smoothed his thumb along her lower lip. "A bit of honey dropped," he told her as the excuse for that caress.

She didn't believe him but she couldn't argue with him either. She could barely speak or move.

"Would you like more?" he asked softly, his eyes caressing exactly where his finger had just touched, making her body tremble even more.

A movement to the right of her caught her attention and she looked around, suddenly realizing that the crowd had stopped to watch the two of them interact.

Her cheeks turned a bright pink and she looked down, horrified at such a lack of decorum on her part. Garon seemed to take pity on her and put his arm around her, bringing her closer so that her face was buried against his chest.

"It is excellent," he told the woman who was beaming, standing beside them as she held more of the decadent delicacy out to them. She nodded all the while, bowing. The elderly woman's delight in offering her ruler something made her whole family pat each other on the back. Her husband bowed as well and offered a whole plate, already wrapped, as a gift. Garon winked at the man and accepted the offering while Layla wanted to punch his arm for being so obvious about his lascivious intent. It was as if the two men were silently agreeing that the honeyed mixture would aid in their wedding night and she wanted to just fall into a hole somewhere.

As they walked on, she was grateful that they were moving to another part of the festival, the area where she didn't have to eat anything any longer. She wasn't sure she could swallow another bite after that last scene so when someone showed her a toy, she eagerly took it and learned how to make the adorable puppet dance. It was the perfect excuse to put several feet of space between herself and Garon, giving her time to recover from his touch. Her lips were still tingling from his fingers and her stomach was weak. Not to mention her mind that was craving things that were completely wrong wrong wrong! And she couldn't seem to stop those treasonous thoughts from entering her mind so she pulled away from him, putting as much space between them as he and the crowds, not to mention the security team, would allow.

She and Garon moved from vendor to vendor, looking at the various items for sale and complimenting each person. She was given gifts by each person and she thanked them, sincerely touched by their desire to be a part of this celebration. And if she felt slightly guilty for accepting what were essentially wedding gifts, she pushed that aside, knowing that all of them were well meant. It was irrelevant that she had absolutely no desire to be married to the man. Apparently, she was hiding that sentiment completely from the crowds.

"Why don't you go over to the dais again and relax now?" he suggested, touching her arm slightly.

She looked towards where he was pointing and saw her mother looking stiff and disapproving. "Where are you going?" she asked, hiding her cringe of distaste at joining her mother's sour presence once again. It wasn't that she wanted to be with him. But she definitely didn't want to be near her mother who would smile as she lectured Layla on anything she felt her daughter needed to improve upon. How that woman could lecture while barely moving her lips was a talent, Layla thought.

"I'm going to participate in the next competition."

She looked startled by that announcement. "What's coming next?" She looked around and realized that there was a shooting match starting up.

"There's rifles and archery next. I won't compete, but the crowd wants me to at least showcase my skills."

Her eyes lit up with that news. "Hmm…" she speculated. And then she made a snap decision. She didn't care if it was right or wrong. "I'll join in the shooting as well."

He laughed softly. "Why would you do that?"

She looked up at him, angry that he doubted her skills. "Why wouldn't I? You're going to. Why not me as well?"

Garon thought it was adorable that she wanted to participate. "If you really want to shoot a rifle or a bow and arrow, I can show you how."

Layla kept her expression clear of any sort of laughter. "Oh, would you? Could you really take the time?" She tried to ensure that there wasn't any sarcasm in her tone, but Garon was starting to get to know this woman a little better.

"You're angry about yesterday, aren't you?" he asked as he led her over to the rifle range which had been carefully set up for maximum safety but also so that as many people as possible could watch their ruler showcase his skills.

He picked up one of the smaller rifles, testing the sights and examining all of the moving parts for safety.

"I don't know what you mean," she replied even while she accepted the rifle.

He ignored that comment but suspected there was some meaning he wasn't grasping. "Turn to the right and pull back your right arm," he commented, his eyes conveying that he knew she was just being diplomatic. "I'm sorry that I was pulled away from our lunch."

She knew in that instant that she'd made a mistake about joining in the shooting exhibition. Instead of just handing her the rifle, Garon was going to show her how to use it. But that also meant he was almost embracing her. His chest pressed against her back while his hands moved her into the correct shooting position. "You have every right to be upset," he told her, pretending to show her the different parts of the rifle. "Did you get my message?"

"The one delivered by a minion of the palace? Of course. He very nicely conveyed your regrets. And I returned the favor."

He chuckled, the sound extremely close to her ear. "I got your message." He shifted her hand closer on the stock of the rifle. "I heard your meaning loud and clear, my beauty."

She let him pretend to explain things to her, even while she tried hard to concentrate. She had to concentrate on both the rifle as well as resisting the man's impact on her focus. She didn't want to look like a fool, but she would if he didn't step away from her.

"Okay, you're ready to shoot. Just pretend that's my face instead of a target and you'll do fine."

Layla couldn't help but laugh and was relieved when he stepped away. She repositioned her arms and body so that she was more comfortable, then leaned her head down, took aim and fired.

"Bulls eye!" he commented, sounding surprised. Then his eyes narrowed on her confident stance. "Was that beginner's luck or have you done this before?"

Layla's eyes changed slightly at his condescending manor. But then she remembered that the press and everyone close was watching so she pasted a bright smile on her face before turning back to the target. Once again, she lined up her sights and fired six more rounds. All of them hitting so close together that the black area of the bull's eye was gone. The crowds cheered wildly and the press went crazy trying to capture Garon's expression which was initially stunned, but then took on a look that revealed how impressed he was with his future bride.

When she turned, she slipped the safety into place and handed him the rifle with a polite smile and what appeared to the press as a respectful curtsy. But in reality, Garon knew that she was mocking him.

He laughed, delighted with her more than he'd thought possible. He knew that most men might not like their women to know how to shoot a rifle, but with her sparkling jewelry, her luxurious black hair pilled on her head with little ringlets on the sides and back that danced whenever she moved, she looked like the complete opposite of a woman who could shoot so well. She was beautiful, sexy and smart. And she could shoot like a pro!

Garon took the rifle and laughed. A moment later, he accepted more bullets from a range guard. After loading the gun, he turned to Layla with a wink. A moment later, he quickly turned and fired the rifle with quick succession. She had no idea what he was doing but someone ran down the range to retrieve the target, handing it to Garon. Garon in turn, bowed as he handed the target to Layla who forced herself to smile and show the crowd. It wasn't just a smiley face. It was a winking smiley face! Which was why he'd winked at her right before firing!

"A wee bit smug, Your Highness," she quipped.

Garon threw back his head and laughed, pulling her close and kissing her forehead. And again, the crowd roared their delight in their teasing even though they couldn't hear what was being said between the two of them.

"Let's watch the competition, shall we?" he suggested, taking her hand and leading her back to the pavilion.

Layla watched with trepidation as she walked beside this man who intimidated her in some ways, excited her in others and angered her almost constantly. But none of those emotions could stop her feet from hesitating when she caught sight of her mother's stern, obviously disapproving expression.

"What's wrong?" Garon asked, feeling the change in her pace before she forced herself to keep moving alongside him.

"Nothing," she whispered, bowing her head.

Garon followed where she'd been looking and caught sight of her mother's glare only moments before the stern woman smoothed her elegant features into a placid expression. "So your mother disapproves, eh?" he commented, low enough so only she could hear.

Layla smothered her sigh of acceptance at her mother's censure. "My mother has never approved of my actions, Your Highness. But she's very proud that I am your final choice for your future."

Garon chuckled. "I'm sensing a great deal of antipathy over that statement. Am I wrong?"

Layla shuttered her eyes. "I'm sure you're smart enough to deduce the truth in most situations, Your Highness."

Garon wanted to do something, anything, to get that teasing smile back onto her beautiful features. She'd been so proud of herself trying to compete with him during the rifle portion of the competitions but now she was tense and back to her previous polite demeanor. And he suspected it was mostly due to the strict eyes of their overly deferential chaperone. He shuddered to think of what had gone on during Layla's youth, but he was proud of the woman she was now. He couldn't think of why she'd turned out so beautifully with such rigid disapproval for most of her life, but he was thankful.

Layla sat on the pavilion as the sun really started to beat down on the events. She focused all of her attention on the competitors but she was grateful when Garon waved over a servant and, a moment later, ice water was delivered to her as well as the other guests sitting in the stand. She thirstily drank down the water, feeling somewhat refreshed afterwards.

When the winner of the shooting competition was announced, Garon handed the medal to her and she stepped down, pinning the medal to the man's shirt. "Congratulations!" she enthused. "Great work."

The man blushed as he bowed down in front of her. "It will be a prodigious honor when you marry our great leader, my lady," he said, then scurried off as if he were embarrassed to have made such an effusive comment.

She turned back to Garon, not sure how he would feel about someone complimenting her. Was he the jealous type? But the look on his face wasn't jealousy. Was that…pride?

He took her hand and led her over to the archery area. There were more people ready to watch this competition and Garon walked up to the range, picked up a bow and arrow, then turned to her. "Are you as good at archery as you are at shooting?" he asked.

Layla considered telling him that she didn't know how to shoot a bow and arrow but with the devilish look in his eyes, she knew that he would simply show her how. Which meant he would wrap his body around hers just as he had done with the rifle "lesson". She couldn't take that. Her nerves were already raw from the day's events and she was painfully aware of the man standing here.

"I can shoot," she told him. Taking the bow from his hands, she also accepted an arm and finger guard, strapping them on before accepting the arrow.

She notched the arrow and ignored the tingling feeling on the back of her neck. She knew Garon was watching her but she focused all of her attention on the target. When she released the arrow, she instantly knew that it hadn't gone into the bull's eye.

"Need some pointers?" Garon asked, as both of them looked at her arrow pointing out of the second circle.

Layla turned to glare at him. "Another arrow, please," she said.

Someone handed her another arrow and she slotted it onto the bow. She was taking aim when she stopped, lowered the bow and shook her head. Slipping her shoes off, she repositioned herself, aimed and fired. The arrow went right to the center of the bull's eye. With that, she nodded her head in satisfaction, then very daintily slipped her shoes back on and smiled gracefully as she handed the bow back to Garon.

The man just chuckled, clapping right along with the roaring crowd. "Very entertaining, my lady," he told her.

She was proud of herself. "Going to make a smiley face with the next ten arrows?" she asked.

He shook his head. "No. But do you think you can do it again?" he asked, taking a bow, aiming and firing. Dead center, of course. He turned back to Layla, his black eyebrow raised in challenge.

"Are you daring me to compete with you?" she asked, her heart accelerating at the enticing prospect.

He shrugged one of his massive shoulders, trying to appear casual but she could see the dare in his eyes. "Unless you're afraid to test your skills against mine," he retorted, adding fuel to the challenge.

Layla gasped! "I'm not afraid of you," she came right back.

He moved closer and she knew from the look in his eyes that the subject had changed. "Yes you are, but we're talking about archery right now. Not the way I make you feel when I touch you."

Layla leaned back, her blue eyes clashing with his dark ones. "I won't let you terrify me," she told him, frowning and trying to pretend like her words were true.

He lifted his hand, his index finger running down her cheek. "Unfortunately, and for some strange reason, I do. But I'm going to change that."

She didn't know what to say in response but somehow, his words eased something inside of her she hadn't known was tense. "Archery is going to do that?" she asked, trying to lighten the mood.

He chuckled at her blatant misunderstanding of the conversation. "It will help. Especially since I'll get to show you some tips. Which means I'll get to touch this incredibly soft skin of yours."

And her body tensed right back up with those words. "That comment is not conducive to helping me trust you."

He chuckled as he stepped back. "Ah, but it throws off your focus, giving me the advantage."

Her eyes narrowed in his direction because he was right. "You're a really horrible man. But if you need that kind of an advantage to beat me," she said, leaving the rest unsaid as she shrugged and walked over to the next target. She turned back to him, unaware of the saucy expression on her face. "You may start first, Your Highness."

He bowed and shook his head. "I would never be so rude. Ladies first," he told her.

She shrugged and lifted the bow, setting the arrow and lifting to aim. She was just about to release the arrow when she stopped and took off her shoes again. Competing in heels was not the best choice. And she was playing to win now.

The score was even, with him having a slightly stronger aim until she saw her mother's glare out of the corner of her eye. She accepted what she needed to do.

With an accuracy born out of hours of practicing, she shot her arrow slightly to the left of the bull's eye.

After that, she missed each of her shots just slightly.

In the end, he won the competition and her heart pounded with resentment that she had to throw the competition. It was probably for the best though. Garon's people needed to know that he was the best. It gave them confidence in his leadership and she honestly didn't want to undermine that in any way. She might not like the arranged marriage, but Garon was leading his people out of a decade of war and bringing the economy back with strength and determination. His people needed that belief more than she needed to win and prove something to Garon.

Garon accepted the win, but his eyes told her that he knew something was wrong. "What happened?" he muttered into her ear as he led her up onto the archery pavilion where they would watch the professionals start their competition.

She smiled and waved to the crowd, all of which were noisily cheering on her efforts and their ruler's skill. "I don't know what you're talking about."

He looked down at her curiously and shook his head. "Yes you do. But we'll discuss that later." He turned around and sat down next to her as the archery competition commenced.

The competitions finished and she was amazed by how proud all of the competitors were to receive their medals from Garon. She stood to the side and applauded all of them but as the festivities started to draw to a close, her nervousness increased. Tonight was the big ball! She would have to dance in his arms and smile as if everything were okay. She wasn't sure she could do that. Not after everything that had happened today. How was she supposed to smile and greet other people while standing beside Garon?

Chapter 4

It was just as bad as she'd anticipated!

He didn't overtly touch her. But every gentle caress distracted her concentration. He sent a message to her while dressing that he didn't want her to wear gloves tonight. She'd just been about to pull them on, hoping for as little touching as possible.

She stared at the gold satin gloves, considering her options. Should she obey him? All of her teachings told her that she should lay those silk gloves down onto her dressing table and walk out gloveless. It was a specific request and she should, if she were a very good person, follow that command.

But in the end, she lifted those gloves and pulled them on. Smiling as she did so.

Was it an act of rebellion? Absolutely, she thought with relish. Garon was doing things to her that she didn't like. Not one little bit. He didn't respect her space, he didn't even bother to ask her if he could kiss her or touch her. It was infuriating, the liberties that man took.

She ignored the almost intimate connection she'd felt earlier in the day with Garon while they were shooting. For a few moments, it had felt as if they were together, facing the world as a team. She'd enjoyed teasing him about her skill at shooting a rifle and she'd been excited to shoot the bow and arrow right alongside him.

But that was when they'd been surrounded by the crowds. It had felt safer when they were in front of crowds, where he couldn't....okay, so he'd ignored the crowds and fed her baklava. That was different. She still couldn't believe how her body had reacted when he'd done that!

There would be only two hundred people at the gala tonight. Normally, that would be an overwhelming crowd for her but facing Garon, she needed a larger gathering. She wanted so many people crowding into the palace ballroom that the two of them would be forced to separate, maybe mingle on opposite sides of the event just so they could meet more people.

Actually, that might not be such a bad idea. The more she thought about it, the more she liked it!

"You're all ready," the stylist said, stepping back to survey her work. "And you look beautiful!"

Layla looked at her image in the mirror and cringed inwardly. She had so much makeup on and, with the stiff hair, she barely recognized herself. What would Garon do when she woke up in the morning after their wedding? She stifled a chuckle at the idea of him not even recognizing her when there wasn't a stylist and makeup artist getting her ready for each event. Oh, that would be hilarious, she thought as she stood up and smoothed her gloves high up on her arms. She could just imagine walking down the palace hallway and right out the front door, with no one being the wiser that it was their ruler's wife that was escaping because she would look so different without all of this heavy makeup and her hair not so tightly caught up in an elaborate style.

And Garon wouldn't even blink in her direction.

She wondered what she might look like after…well, their wedding night. With all of this makeup still on and her hair no longer stiff, how would she look without her usual shower and scrubbing at night?

Or maybe they would sleep in separate quarters? Her parents did.

She breathed a sigh of relief at that possibility. Separate bedrooms made sense. At least in her mind. Although, the way he kept touching her, she wasn't sure if he was thinking in the same direction.

Layla sighed. This whole mess was such a confusing problem. If only he would act appropriately, she wouldn't feel so unbalanced when they were together!

If she could figure out how to keep her distance, she was fairly sure that she could form her own life, get her own priorities established and…

They were walking down the hallway, her in the front and her parents directly behind her with their bodyguards flanking the group when she spotted him. He literally took her breath away, just as he had two nights ago. He looked magnificent, she thought, not even aware that she'd stopped in the middle of the hallway.

Garon watched her and she could almost feel those eyes traveling up and down her body. That annoying trembling started up once again. He had that look in his eyes that told her he was once again in predator mode, stalking his prey. And she was the prey he was after.

Taking her gloved hand, he lifted it higher. His hand touching the gloves while his eyes looked down into hers. "Obviously, you did not receive my message," he said so softly that only she could hear his words. His nimble fingers were already working the gloves off of her hands and Layla wanted so badly to curl her fingers into a fist so that he couldn't finish removing that barrier.

"I got your message," she replied defiantly.

His answering smile made the muscles in her stomach clench in an odd way. "That makes it so much better then." The laughter in his eyes caused her teeth to clench furiously.

"I want my gloves on," she almost snapped but hid enough of her anger at the last moment so the words came out more politely.

"And I want them off," he came right back. He moved closer. "Who do you think is going to win?"

Of course he won and he handed the gloves to the man standing behind him, not even bothering to look. His dark eyes held her blue ones captive, just as he was doing to her body. Did he even know the sensations that were zinging through her? Could he tell what she was feeling?

She certainly hoped not. Layla took a step back, dropping her eyes. She'd lost both the battle for her gloves as well as the silent contest and she hated herself for backing down. But there was just something about the man that made her react in strange ways. And she hated him for it!

"Now we'll start this greeting over again, properly." Garon lifted her hand to his mouth in what others would perceive as a gallant gesture.

But did he give her just a simple kiss as a gentleman would do? Absolutely not! His lips kissed her fingers and then his teeth nibbled her fingertips. Goodness, shock and sensation spiked down her body, pooling in that embarrassing place that she'd never realized existed!

She tried to pull her hand away but he wouldn't allow it.

"No gloves." His eyes fired up.

She lowered her lashes, wishing she could hide herself as easily as she could hide her eyes. "I didn't realize that your message was an order," she replied back.

He chuckled. "It wasn't an order, so much as a desire to hold your hand without gloves to hinder my touch of your soft skin." He tucked her hand onto his arm and they started walking towards the gala.

Layla looked over at the closed doorway just as the guards were about to open them. "I will have to remember that your commands are actually optional," she commented.

The doors opened and that's when he let the bomb drop. "Oh, they're not optional, my beauty," he said as they stepped up to the landing. They stood still for several moments, letting the press take pictures before they started to descend the stairs to join the guests when he continued, "I thoroughly enjoy the consequences when you don't follow them."

Layla almost stumbled with those words. Thankfully, he was anticipating just such a reaction and held her steady. She looked at the crowd, praying that the two of them were the only ones that had noticed the slip.

"I can't believe you just said that," she replied when they were halfway down the staircase and she had some of her composure back. They were practically alone on the stairs, the press still clicking away, the lights flashing madly while they descended. "Of all the rude and inappropriate comments you've conveyed to me, that has to be the worst." And she said all of it with a smile, refusing to let the rest of the world know that her intended husband was now on her black list. Well, he'd actually been on that list the whole time, but at the moment, he was the only person there. She was furious with him. But not really sure if he was teasing her or not.

"Believe it," he responded and pulled her closer. "We will dance now."

And with that, he pulled her onto the dance floor. Nodding curtly to the orchestra, he took her hand in his and laid her other hand on his shoulder, knowing she was too shocked to do it for herself. Or angry. Either way, he wasn't giving up this moment with her. He wanted to dance, to hold her close, to feel that energy surging through her. When the music started, he pulled her into the dance.

Layla hadn't anticipated any of this. Not his comments or the dance. Of course, she'd known she would dance with him. But this wasn't dancing. Not really, she thought as she stared at the middle of his chest, surprised by how easily he moved across the parquet floor. It was almost as if they were floating. Her full skirt swirled like a soft, silken cloud around his legs and he guided her around effortlessly.

"Look at me," Garon told her softly, but with a tone that conveyed he would not be disobeyed.

Layla stiffened even more in his arms. "I don't think I will, Your Highness," she said with a smile as she glanced out at the crowd. She was silently telling him that she would look at everyone but him.

"Layla, you really don't want to challenge me here, my love." He pulled her closer, so close that her breasts were almost touching his chest. "There are so many things I could do right now that would..." He chuckled as her pretty eyes snapped up to him. "That's better." He pulled her closer anyway.

She gasped when his hand moved lower on her back. "You said if I looked at you..."

"Yes, but you still tested my authority."

She narrowed her eyes at him. "And you have absolute authority over me, don't you?"

His black eyebrows went up with those words. "Is that what is bothering you, love?" he asked gently. "Are you feeling powerless?"

Layla looked away, refusing to give him even more power. "I'm perfectly fine," she told him.

But that was a complete lie. And he knew it. Layla shivered in his arms and he bent his head closer to her. She could feel his breath on her shoulder, on her ear and…No! She didn't like that feeling! Not one little bit.

So why did she sigh when he pulled her even closer? This was all so confusing, she thought and closed her eyes as he twirled her around the dance floor. For such a large man, he could move wonderfully. She couldn't help herself when she relaxed ever so slightly in his arms. It just felt too nice. She'd never partnered with a man who could move with such effortless grace and still look masculine.

All of her expectations about this man, her marriage and her future were tumbling down around her feet in chaos. Layla had been told from an early age what to expect, how to act, how to react…but the past few days have blown away all of those lessons. She couldn't figure out what was expected of her, how to react. She'd been told all her life that she should anticipate problems so embarrassment could be avoided. But how does one anticipate the strange and unpredictable feelings that Garon stirred within her?

She almost sagged with relief when the others started moving onto the dance floor. And for several moments, she relaxed in Garon's arms. He pulled her closer now that they were no longer on display and she sighed, wishing she could lay her head down against his chest. It had been such a long, stressful day, much of it brought on by this man. But there was just something about his arms around her right now that….well, she liked it. And it felt…safe? Ever since meeting this man, she'd felt decidedly not-safe. So all the more reason to take this moment and relish this non-threatening instant.

Garon held this slender woman in his arms and, for the first time since meeting her, he felt her relax ever so slightly. She was always so stiff and formal, so nervous. But never timid! No, he smiled as he pulled her slightly closer, his fiancée was never timid. A fact which he liked.

He almost laughed at the way she'd shown up tonight wearing those golden gloves. He'd loved pulling them off of her hands. Just as he was thoroughly anticipating sliding her wedding dress from her body, revealing every inch of her soft, beautiful skin to his hungry eyes.

Garon pulled back from that image because his body simply couldn't take any more stimulation. Besides, Layla was in his arms and he could feel her soft breath against his neck, feel her full breasts pressing against his chest and she wasn't trying to get away from him. It was a novel experience and he wasn't going to do anything to change this moment. He even ignored his aide when the man gestured for him. Garon knew that he should take Layla's hand and start introducing her around to the various dignitaries. For the first time in his adult life, he was ignoring his responsibilities in favor of simply enjoying the moment.

There would be enough time after this dance to introduce her around. This was their moment, he told himself. And he wasn't stopping it for anything.

Chapter 5

Layla stood in Garon's office, pacing back and forth. The scene was similar to yesterday's when she'd been waiting for him after his summons. But today was different in that she'd requested a meeting with him.

His aide had immediately agreed to the meeting but cautioned her that "His Highness" was trying to complete business before the wedding. He ushered her into Garon's office, letting her know that he would inform "His Highness" that she was waiting for him, wishing to speak with him about an urgent matter.

Layla wasn't sure it was urgent, but she was glad that the other man thought so. And the time it took to retrieve her fiancé gave her a bit more time to compose her thoughts. She was furious with him over their encounters yesterday, all of them ending with last night's gala. The way he'd touched her, caressed her, fed her foods and created an atmosphere in which he tried to portray that theirs was a love story...well, it infuriated her!

She couldn't believe how she'd stood in his arms, actually enjoying the way he felt with his strength surrounding her, his hands touching her so gently.

She rubbed her forehead, trying to regain her perspective. This was wrong! Everything was wrong! Her pacing continued, becoming more impatient as the minutes passed.

"Good morning, my beauty," Garon said several minutes later as he stepped into his office and closed the door.

"Open it back up!" she whispered angrily, her whole body shaking with that strange, foreign emotion that had only grown stronger now that he was in the room.

The door clicked shut with a snick and he leaned against it, crossing his arms over his chest as he watched her hands form fists at her sides. "I gather you are upset about something?" he observed.

"Yes! Why are you acting like this?" she demanded.

His dark eyebrows went up in surprise. "Like a man about to be married?" he offered.

"No!" she closed her eyes and shook her head slightly. "I mean, yes! But..." she almost growled with frustration. "You know what I'm talking about."

He pushed away from the door and moved closer to her. "I'm not sure I do understand. Why don't you enlighten me?" Every interlude with this woman added to the complexity of who she was. Yesterday, she'd shown him that she was more than just a pretty face. She could shoot, charm the crowds as well as himself and still look stunning doing all of it with confidence and a gracious manner that made his people fall in love with her. Then last night, she'd stood in his arms, almost caressing him with her breath and shown how vulnerable she really was. And how soft.

Now she was practically spitting flames of anger. The changes in her were fascinating and he couldn't wait to see what she was like in bed. Was she all soft and cuddly? Or would she light the sheets of fire with her passion?

Layla recognized the way he was looking at her and stepped back, putting one of the large chairs between them. She wanted it both to hold herself up as well as to fight the need to rush over to him and punch her fists against his hard chest. "You know what's happening and you have to stop it! This isn't right! You're acting..."

"As if I enjoy my fiancée's company?" he filled in when she seemed to stumble over the words.

"Yes! You have to stop that!"

He suppressed the urge to laugh. "Why is that?"

Her hands fisted at her sides in frustration at his pretense of misunderstanding what she was trying to say. "Because you're giving the world the impression that this is a love match when it is the farthest thing from it! We will have an arranged marriage. We don't even like each other!"

"I like you." He had to fight to keep his eyes from moving down her delectable figure. He suspected that would infuriate her even further.

She stomped her foot at his reaction as well as the heat that had suddenly appeared in his eyes. "You don't even know me!"

"Isn't that what all of this is about?" he suggested.

She glared at him before she shook her head. "No!" Yes! What was her point?

"Tell me what we're doing then?"

She wanted to pull her hair out! Why was he being like this? Why wasn't he acting in an expected manner? "We have an arranged marriage. It is a political union! We should be presenting ourselves to your people and the world as such!" She'd started out in what she'd thought was a calm tone of voice but ended almost yelling at him.

"And what should we be doing differently?" he asked.

How could he even ask that? Wasn't it obvious? "No touching! Royal couples do not touch! They might hold hands occasionally, but they don't touch! They don't caress! They don't do that..." she raised her hands out in front of herself and wiggled her fingers, stammering to describe what he'd done yesterday, "nibble or whatever that was last night. They do not feed each other, they don't..." She stopped because she didn't want to reveal anything else to him for fear of giving him ammunition.

"Kiss?" he suggested softly but with that deep, sexy voice. And his eyes dropped to her lips, caressing them with his gaze.

She gasped, frozen in place for a long moment before she snapped out of it. Her fingers were gripping the back of the chair so tightly that her knuckles were turning white. "No! They never kiss! They don't do that sort of thing! Ever!"

"How are we to produce an heir then?" he laughed.

She stomped her foot. "Don't even suggest such a thing! You have no idea all the silly tests I was required to endure!"

His eyes snapped to hers. "Tests? What tests?"

She backed away. "Don't you dare pretend you don't know! Your staff required all of those tests. I had to see several specialists to ensure my fertility! I endured numerous exams, my weight was compared to my BMI, one doctor even suggested that I should gain five point three pounds in order to be at my optimal weight for becoming pregnant!"

A curious look entered those dark eyes and he stopped moving closer to her. "Tell me." What kinds of tests could be so bad that she was embarrassed to discuss them? His imagination immediately took a turn that he instinctively knew she wouldn't like.

She shook her head, her cheeks turning pink at the memories. "No."

"Why not?"

"Because I had to live through them once. There's nothing you can say that will make me live through them again, even if only by telling you what I was required to do."

He considered her words for a moment, then nodded, accepting her answer. "And you won't let me make it all worthwhile?"

She took a deep breath and once again tried to calm down. His question sounded as if he were going to be reasonable about this scenario. "You can. By not touching me in public. Don't touch me, don't do that...thing...with your eyes. Don't do all of that...stuff! You've been doing it since we met three days ago and it..." she paused for a moment. "It. Has. To. Stop!" Her hand sliced through the air with each word.

Damn, she was beautiful when she was furious like this. Oh, and she was telling him what to do. He loved it when she tried that. It just got all of his predatory instincts into overdrive and all he wanted to do was lift her into his arms, carry her over to his desk so that he could lay her out and show her who was in charge in the most erotic way possible. "And if I don't?" he asked in a deceptively calm voice.

Layla shivered. "Well, then..." she wasn't sure what her ultimatum might be. "Then I'll just have to back out of this. I'll tell the press that I couldn't be the woman you need."

"Ah, but that would be a lie,' he said with a silky smooth tone.

"It isn't a lie!" she almost shouted. "I'm not the kind of woman you think I am! I'm not..."

His smile was so slight that, if she weren't looking at him at that exact moment, she might have missed it. "I'm going to prove you wrong, so be careful about whatever statement you're about to make," he cautioned.

She was visibly shaking now. "You're not listening to me!" she snapped, losing control as he stepped closer to her. The chair was no barrier and she hated her weakness.

"I heard every word you said." He grabbed her wrist when she tried to keep the chair between them, pulling her closer. With a flick of his hands, the chair was gone and she was plastered against his chest, one arm around her back, pressing her closer while she tried to push away from the intimacy of this embrace. "You said no touching," and his free hand moved up to trail a line of fire down her cheek. "And no nibbling," his mouth latched onto her earlobe, biting the tender flesh that no man had ever touched. "And no caressing," he finished off as his hand moved down her arm, lifting her hand so that it was on his shoulder while he looked down into her blue eyes that were both fearful and filling with desire. "And no kissing."

She gasped, her eyes watching with terror as his head descended once again. She shook her head, trying to tell him no but his hand moved to her hair, diving into the dark tresses and holding her head still.

She couldn't breathe as she waited for that moment when his mouth would touch hers. Layla couldn't have anticipated the wave of sensation that roared through her when the touch finally came. It was as if a tidal wave of desire swept over her, sucking her into a need so strong, she whimpered with confusion even as her body melted against his. The hand gripping her hair pulled her head back further so he could deepen the kiss and Layla's hands gripped his shoulders, unaware of the embrace and only aware of this kiss, his lips as they moved over her mouth. When his tongue slid across her lips, she almost pulled back, but his teeth nipped her lower lip and she gasped, giving him access to her mouth. His tongue took full advantage of that slip, diving into the warm, moist heat of her mouth, mating with hers, teasing her tongue to participate in the kiss.

Layla wasn't sure what to do so she imitated his movements, wanting more but not sure what that more might be, or even how to ask for it. All she knew was that this man was doing things to her that she didn't understand but didn't want to stop either.

Unfortunately, he lifted his head and looked down at her. "What were you saying?" he asked, his hands sliding up and down her back, one hand going so low, it rested against her bottom.

Layla realized what was happening, that he'd just kissed her senseless. And she'd kissed him back!

Jerking out of his arms, she stepped backwards, wiping the back of her hand against her mouth as if she could wipe the kiss off. But the effects of that kiss weren't on the outside. They were inside where her body was still clamoring for him to kiss her again, wanting him to touch her with his hands and go to the next step.

"How dare you!" she gasped, horrified both at him for his audacity as well as herself for her complete lack of conviction and self-discipline. "Don't..."

"Careful what you say Layla," he cautioned as he moved closer to her once again. "The last time you tried to lay down the law, you ended up in my arms. And if you do that again, I promise that I won't stop with just a kiss."

Her hands moved up to cover her mouth and that action only caused amusement to appear in his eyes. "Don't..." she started to say, raising her hand up higher when he stepped closer again. "I won't..."

Layla wasn't sure what to say or what to do. She'd never been in this kind of a situation before. Sure, men had stolen kisses from her over the years. But never had they affected her like this one had! Never had she been so lost in a kiss that she'd completely given over control. If someone had walked in on them...!

"What if my mother had found us like that?" she demanded.

Garon stared at her for a moment, wondering if she realized what she'd just said. When he saw the completely serious expression in her eyes, he threw back his head and laughed.

Layla stared at him, not quite sure what was happening. He was laughing at her? He thought her predicament was funny? How dare he!

She stepped up to him, her anger rising to fury and she pounded him on the chest, letting all of her anger and this pent up frustration out as she let loose on him. "Don't you dare laugh at me!" she almost yelled. "There is nothing funny about this situation! You're just a horrible man!"

Garon felt the jabs but she wasn't hurting him. Not in the least. He suspected that his darling fiancée was actually holding back because these paltry punches were nothing compared to what he suspected she might be capable of. But he knew that she was genuinely angry with him. Well, not angry, but sexually frustrated. And she didn't understand how to deal with that frustration. He knew that she was a virgin and, beyond that, she was innocent of men. So he didn't take offense when she tried to hit him. But he did wrap his arm around her waist, pulling her against him once more. The action stopped her punches and, since his arm was pressing her whole body against his, she was suddenly aware of the affect her anger had on him. Well, her anger, her kisses, her soft body against his…it all added up to the expected reaction.

She tried to pull away but he wouldn't let her. His hands moved lower, his fingers spreading out onto her bottom as he pressed her more fully against his erection. "Get used to it, Layla," he told her, his voice gravelly. "You've been doing this to me since the first moment I laid eyes on you. It's time you faced up to the reality of life. You're mine," he told her. "And if your mother were to walk in here and catch us kissing, or holding or even me touching you in any way, she has no authority here. We're already going to be married in two days. You will be my wife and we will explore this more fully. And I promise," he said as his hand moved from her bottom to slide softly down her cheek, "we will be doing so much more once we are married. And you'll discover that this anger you're feeling is only sexual frustration and it will go away once we…"

She covered his mouth with her hand, not wanting to hear him say the word. She jerked out of his arms and stepped away. "I'm so relieved that you think just…doing that…" she spat out, "will help me get over my anger at being sold into marriage with you. But I have news for you, Your Highness," she said with a sneer, "I don't like you. I don't want to be married to you. I know that I don't have a choice, that both of our countries need this marriage, but I'm not going to be that silly little girl that comes to your bed all eager and excited. No! I'll be your wife. But…"

"Don't say it, Layla," he told her, trying to be stern and not chuckle at her anger. She was just so beautiful when she was spouting off treason like this. His body hardened even more, aching to show her the wonders of the marriage bed. Just two more days, he promised himself.

She huffed angrily, too furious to say anything more. So instead of giving him a good piece of her mind since her mind had obviously gone somewhere else, she stormed out of his office, slamming the door behind her.

Garon watched her go, thinking about calling her back and finishing that interlude with a bit more satisfaction. He eyed his large desk and contemplated all the delights he could show her. But he sighed and rubbed a hand over his face, trying to tamp down the lust that was still rampaging through his own body. One thing was certain, he said as he let his aide know that they could start the next meeting, his marriage was certainly going to be interesting. He would never be bored.

Layla walked back to the suite of rooms she'd been sleeping in, trying hard to tamp down her fury. She felt like she was going to explode with anger at any moment. She must have looked it too because the servants took one look at her face and bowed out of the room.

And that made her even more angry. She didn't want people to be afraid of her. But she was actually afraid of herself right at the moment.

She pulled on workout clothes and once again, headed for the gym. After an hour of running, she felt slightly better. She'd worked off a great deal of her anger and she was ready for whatever came next. She pressed the end button on the treadmill and grabbed a towel, wiping off the perspiration as her breathing slowed down.

"You're late for your final fittings," her mother snapped as soon as Layla stepped into the suite.

Layla looked at her mother, curious about her life. "Mother, are you happy?" she asked.

Her mother sighed. "Happiness is not important. What is important is getting to your fittings on time." She glanced down at her watch pointedly. "And you have thirty minutes. There won't be any time to do your hair and nails, much less your makeup."

Layla looked down at her nails. "There's nothing wrong with my manicure," she commented but should have kept her mouth shut.

"It is the wrong color!" her mother explained with impatience.

Layla didn't respond. She walked into the shower and closed the door, shutting out her mother and her ridiculous notions about life and what was important. Of course happiness was important. That was the entire point of being alive. It was why people worked fifty weeks out of every year just so they could afford a vacation for those other two weeks where they could take off to the forests or camping. It was why people ate chocolate or drank martinis, why they flew to exotic places to see amazing sight from nature. And it was why people fell in love.

Well, she could accomplish all of them but one for her life.

At least one good thing would come from her wedding. Her mother would fly back to their country with her father. Of course, that would leave her alone with Garon, but she would eventually figure out a way to deal with him. Obviously, she'd failed in her efforts today. She shuddered as she remembered how he'd touched her and kissed her. That had been wrong on so many levels. She was a lady. Ladies simply did not feel things like that for their husbands. They were basically business partners. Not lovers.

She quickly showered and dressed, trying to find something that would be easy to take off and on so that the fitting appointment would be easier and more efficient. Layla had two more days of relative freedom. That realization struck her as terrifying. And really, it was only one more day because she would be wed by the second day.

She pulled on a pink blouse and black slacks along with a pretty pair of flowered shoes. The buttons on the blouse would help during the fittings so her hair wouldn't get messed up pulling on and off the dresses, nor would her makeup accidentally come off onto her clothes. A very important trick her mother had taught her growing up. Layla couldn't count the number of hours she'd spent in boutiques trying on one outfit after another while her mother surveyed her figure, examined her complexion in various lights against the color of the outfit and goodness, don't get her started on the shoe shopping! Layla would be perfectly happy if she never had to try on another pair of shoes for the rest of her life. "Shoes are the cornerstone of one's wardrobe!" her mother would say constantly. Or even better, "A good pair of shoes is like an underline on a perfectly worded quote. It brought attention to the positive!"

Layla knew that she was almost a traitor to her gender because of her shoe hatred. But what was a woman to do? She'd spent hours, literally hours some weeks, trudging from one shoe store to another, trying to find the perfect shoe for different outfits. It was almost a religion for her mother.

But that was the reality for one in the public eye, she supposed. The press photographed her mother and father constantly and that would be even worse for Layla now that she was going to marry a sheik. Perhaps it wouldn't be so bad though. Wouldn't the shoe retailers come to her? Or even better, wouldn't she have someone who does all the shopping for her? Oh, goodness, that would be wonderful!

She slumped down on a satin covered chair in her suite, her mind whirling with the realization that she would be someone's wife. Garon's wife! His wife in two days! That gave her less than forty-eight hours!

"Layla!" her mother snapped.

Layla jerked out of her reverie and stood up. Squaring her shoulders, she walked out of her suite and down the long hallway where the designers and seamstresses had been diligently working on the final touches of her new wardrobe.

"Good morning!" the designer, a lady by the name of Giana, clapped her hands as soon as Layla entered. "Are you excited? Only two more days!"

Layla smiled weakly, so overwhelmed by the idea that she couldn't even work up a fake happy attitude for her nuptials. "I can hardly believe it," she lied. She could believe it. She could because this was what she'd been raised to do. What she hadn't anticipated during all of those lessons on comportment, history and politics, was having a man like Garon for her husband. Although, really…no one could have prepared her for a man like Garon. He was…

"Good morning, ladies," Garon's deep voice said from the doorway as he strode confidently and arrogantly into the area reserved exclusively for women.

Layla swung around, her blue eyes wide with horror as she watched him casually enter the dressing area. Did he care that he was entering a sacred area? Not in the slightest! He just walked in as if he owned the place!

Well, she supposed that he actually did own the area. And the room, the palace and…good grief, one could argue that he owned everything! Anything he didn't own, he ruled.

That didn't matter right now though. He should respect this area. He should respect some small aspects of a woman's life that needed to remain private!

"What are you doing here?" she demanded as politely as possible despite the fact that her heart had skipped into overdrive as she took in his broad shoulders and his long legs that carried him into the room with an arrogance that was both impressive and astounding. The calming effects of her run a few hours ago had disappeared and her temper was once again boiling over. Out of the corner of her eye, she saw the shocked expression on Giana's face as well as the horror of the other seamstresses. "You can't be in here. You'll ruin the surprise of my wedding dress!" They were all too surprised by his presence and not sure how to tell him to get out.

When she said those words, the ladies looked much more relieved, some of them even nodding their heads as they agreed with her assertion that the wedding finery should be protected until the wedding day.

"So keep the dress hidden," he said, walking right up to her. As he towered over her, she refused to back away. "I want to see the rest. I need to make sure that you will be adequately draped in the most beautiful materials once we are wed."

Layla fisted her hands at her sides, but hid them behind her back so that he couldn't see how angry he was making her. "I can assure you that these ladies have been working diligently to ensure that you will not be embarrassed with me by your side."

He lifted his hand, running a finger down her neck and smiling when she shivered. "I trust your fashion sense. But there might be things I want to add."

Her eyes widened with that declaration and her heart fluttered annoyingly once more. "I doubt you'll be disappointed," she replied, thinking of all those sheer and lacy bits that the designer had already created. Things she hadn't objected to before her first meeting with this man. Now however…

Garon's hand froze. "Is that a promise?" he asked.

She opened her mouth to respond, but the words couldn't come. Her mind was racing, thinking of all of the sexy clothes Giana had insisted on creating. When she'd first seen them, she had blushed but knew that they were normal for a wedding trousseau. Unfortunately, after being around Garon, understanding this crazy sexual need that she was determined to fight, she didn't want those outfits to come out of their tissue paper wrappings. She didn't want to parade around Garon in those things. He didn't need any additional enticement!

She opened her mouth to tell him no, that she wouldn't be keeping those clothes. But the words wouldn't come. Especially when his thumb came up and rubbed gently against her lower lip.

"I'm looking forward to it," he told her, a promise in that look that tightened her tummy and caused her breath to hitch in her throat.

He turned his head and caught sight of a sheer, purple fabric. He lifted the bolt of fabric up and looked over at her. "Has this been used for anything?" he asked.

Layla's mouth dropped open but in shock this time and her body started shivering when he came up behind her. With one hand he held the end of the fabric but dropped the roll to the floor, draping the sheer material over her figure. "I would love to see your body draped with this fabric," he said softly into her ear. "Would you do that? For me?"

She opened her mouth, wanting to tell him no, but then his chest shifted against her back and she inhaled sharply, closing her eyes to try and fight that pull, the same pull that had gotten her kissed earlier this morning. The same pull that had been creating such a furious response in her every time he touched her.

She suspected that, to the rest of the people in the room, the embrace looked relatively innocent except for the fact that the man was asking for an outfit to be made that would reveal her body to his hungry eyes. What they didn't know was that he was pressing himself against her, his body's response to their conversation obvious to her since it was now pressing against her bottom.

She couldn't look at herself in the mirror, didn't want to see the way he was almost embracing her as he held the purple fabric against her figure, his arms touching her in places that she'd never been touched before. "There are others in the room, Your Highness," she said, hoping that would tamp down what he was doing to her.

Not a chance! "Everyone out of here. Now," he ordered.

The women scurried out of the room. Mere seconds after he'd issued the command, Layla was alone with Garon, held captive in his arms by the material in front of her and his hard, tall, muscular body behind her.

"You shouldn't have done that," she whispered, biting her lower lip to try and fight him.

"Why not?" he asked, the hand holding the fabric was now holding her as well, his hands moving across her stomach in a caress that was very far from innocent.

When his hand moved lower and lower, she waited tensely, wondering what he was going to do. How far would he dare? She wasn't aware of the way her body arched ever so slightly, silently encouraging his bold touch. Nor was she aware of the way she'd stopped breathing, everything inside of her trying to anticipate what he was going to do.

She gasped when his hand slipped inside her slacks and she almost fell to the ground when she felt his fingers against the skin of her stomach. She grabbed his wrist, trying to stop his hand from moving lower but he was stronger than she was. And when his fingers touched the light hair…and lower…all she could do was stand in his arms with her eyes closed and accept the caress, breathless to feel something more.

A noise burst through the sensual haze and she jerked back, out of his arms. She saw the woman with her arms loaded with new fabrics and Layla wasn't sure who was more startled, herself or the seamstress as she stared at the two other occupants of the room.

"I'm so sorry," she stammered out, stepping back out of the room and closing the door.

Layla was so horrified by what had almost happened that she swung around, her eyes blazing fire at Garon. "You….!" She tried to think of something to say that would wipe that confident, triumphant look off of his face. She was shaking so badly, both from what she'd almost allowed him to do as well as from being caught letting him touch her like that.

"That's it! This wedding is off!" she cried, her whole body shaking with both his touch and what she'd just dared to say. But she didn't care! She was finished. "I won't marry a man who doesn't respect me and you obviously don't respect me at all! I can't believe what…" she closed her mouth, unable to say anything about what had just happened.

Instead, she shook her head. "It's over! I don't care about the political repercussions! I'm not marrying you and there's nothing you can say to make me!"

With that, she ran out of the room, slamming the door behind her.

Garon watched her for a stunned moment before her words sunk into his lust-filled mind. "Like hell!" he snapped. She wasn't the only one that was trying to deal with sexual frustration. If she hadn't just threatened to call off the wedding, he might have been able to deal with her more rationally. But the idea of that woman getting out of this palace without him was simply not going to happen. That threat alone doomed her fate as it fired up his temper.

His long legs followed her, eating up the distance. He was out of control now, wanting to finish this and show her that she damn well was his woman and there wasn't anything either of them could do about it. This had nothing to do with politics or agreements. This had everything to do with claiming the woman that had gotten under his skin in just a few days.

She wanted to throw out threats? He'd damn well eliminate that possibility! When he caught up with her, he didn't even stop and explain his intentions. He simply spun her around by the arm and, while she stood there gaping at him, he tossed her over his shoulder and carried her in the opposite direction. When he reached his private suite, his guards already had the door open for him. He kicked it shut a split second before she realized what he'd done and started screaming.

He didn't care. He was through with patience and taking things slowly. He was going to show this woman that they were meant for each other if it was the last thing he did.

Just inside the door, he dropped Layla back down onto her feet. She tried to run, but he already had a hold on her arm and he pulled her into his arms. When she turned her head away, he simply captured her neck. And when her knees gave out on her, he caught her into his arms again.

One moment, Layla was livid that this man would dare to touch her in such a manner. But the next moment his lips and his teeth sank into her neck, she lost it. Her arms wrapped around his neck and her body pressed against his. When his hands tangled in her hair, turning her head back so that he could kiss her, she was more than ready for his kiss. She still might not know how to kiss him well, but what she lacked in experience, she more than made up for in passion. Layla's mind had stopped working. Her body was completely in charge. A small part of her knew that what they were doing was wrong, that she shouldn't want this. But that part of her was ignored as the larger portion of herself was intent on conquering this man.

Her hands were wrapped around his neck but he took them down and she whimpered, needing that contact. But he wouldn't let her, trapping her hands behind her back. "Please, Garon!" she gasped. She didn't understand. She needed to touch him, to feel his hair and the skin of his neck under her fingertips. Since he wouldn't let her touch him with her hands, she lifted her leg up and almost screamed when his body fit against hers more perfectly. Her hips cradled that hard, mysterious part of him more perfectly and she pressed against that part, instinctively needing him against her softness. She pressed and shifted, hearing him growl but not understanding why he made that sound. Her world was all about sensation, of satisfying this aching, desperate need inside of her that she didn't understand.

A moment after her hands were trapped behind her, his other hand came to her silk blouse and ripped. The torn shreds of her blouse hung down on either side of her while his hand moved up to cup her breast. Layla screamed at this new onslaught and pressed her breast into his hand. She felt crazy now. Out of control. When his thumb rubbed against her lace covered nipple, she screamed again. "Please Garon!" she begged, whimpering again.

Garon responded by lifting her up into his arms, his hands cradling her bottom. While he carried her through his suite to his bedroom, his mouth latched onto her nipple, biting and sucking, torturing the peaked flesh with his mouth. Layla hung onto his neck and arched into his mouth, needing more, demanding more even though she wasn't completely sure what 'more' might be. Garon took the strap of her bra between his teeth and pulled it down even while he laid her down on his bed. When the plump flesh was revealed to him, he took her nipple into his mouth, reveling in the mouth to skin contact now.

He was hard and aching for her again, but this time he wasn't pulling back. She'd gone too far with that latest threat and he was going to ensure that she didn't have any possible way of backing out of this wedding. If he'd been thinking clearly, he might have realized what he was about to do was wrong. That it would be right and good in two days but he was out of his mind with need for this woman. He wanted her with a craving beyond anything he'd ever experienced before and he wasn't going to pull back.

He wanted her. She writhed underneath him and he deftly released the closure on her slacks. Standing up, he ripped them off of her legs and then discarded his own shirt, ignoring buttons in favor of expediency. His eyes never left her body and he was so turned on as he looked down at the woman with desire-glazed eyes, one breast out of her lacey bra and a see through bit of nothing covering the apex of her thighs. This was his woman, he thought as he stripped out of his clothes. This was his wife!

He saw her open her mouth and thought she might be about to protest. He wasn't going to let her. He moved back down, holding himself over her as his mouth captured hers, his teeth and tongue making love to her in ways that ensured that she was just as lost as he was in this process.

With a swift, almost angry move, he ripped the lace of her underwear away. There was still a bit of shyness when he did that but he wasn't going to allow anything less than the absolute, uncontrolled passion that had gotten them to this point. They were meant to be together. By some freak of fate, he'd negotiated to have the perfect woman for him as his wife and, from this moment onward, there would be nothing hidden between them. His hands were gentle but firm as he pushed her knees apart, his hand slipping down to caress her thighs before returning to her heat. When he slipped one finger inside of her, he could barely breathe as he realized how wet she was, how ready for him.

He was able to pull back only slightly, remembering that this woman was a virgin and he had to be careful.

Layla didn't want careful! She didn't want to take this slowly! His fingers were magical and when she felt that invasion in her core, she lifted her hips up, her mouth opening with shock at how amazing it felt! She wanted more but wasn't sure how to ask for it. Her hands lifted, trying to reach for him and he took her hand, placing it on his chest. As her fingers eagerly explored, so did his and she shifted her head back and forth, her body arching into his hands. When his thumb touched that extra sensitive bud, she couldn't hold back her reaction. She splintered apart even while her legs wrapped around his waist, needing his body, his strength.

She'd barely come down from that when she felt a probing, something thicker and more powerful. She opened her eyes, her breathing frantic as Garon pressed himself into her heat.

"What...?" she asked, her hands moving from his chest to his arms, her fingers gripping his bulging biceps while he continued to slip in and out of her, going deeper each time.

"You feel so perfect, Layla," he growled, bending down lower to nibble on her neck. "Open for me, love," he coaxed. Garon didn't wait for her compliance. He pushed her legs wider and pressed himself in deeper, watching her face to make sure he didn't hurt her in any way. When she only arched her back again, taking him deeper, he breathed a sigh of relief, knowing that she was still right here with him.

He felt her resistance and almost cursed at the need to break through it. Sweat was forming on his forehead but he couldn't pull back. Not now. And probably not since the moment she'd uttered those words in the seamstress' room.

He gathered her close, kissing her lips and pressed past the presence of her virginity, taking her gasp of pain into his mouth, trying in the only way he knew how to soothe her body.

When she started kissing him back, the feverish pitch that had been there before his invasion, came raging back between them. He couldn't get enough of this woman, wanting all of her and he wouldn't let her hold back either. When she closed her eyes, he stopped moving.

"Open your eyes, Layla," he commanded, his big body shaking as he held onto his control with every ounce of self-discipline he'd ever had. When she didn't immediately obey him, he shouted to her. "Open your eyes!"

She gasped when he started to pull out of her body and she grabbed his hips, her legs clamping around him but she opened her eyes, staring up at him with a confused, worried and lust filled gaze. She wanted to speak, to beg him to continue but she wasn't sure how to speak right at the moment. Every thought, every part of her body was concentrating on this man and the part of him that was intimately connected to her.

So when he moved again, she moaned out his name. Lifting her hips, needing something, her body tightening for that incredible release she'd just experienced and not sure how to get it again.

"I don't..." she started to say but he pressed into her. Faster and faster, he moved in and out of her, spiraling her need to higher and higher depths. "Garon, I can't..." she started to say but then his hand slid down her stomach, his thumb touched that part of her that seemed swollen and needy and when he pressed into her again, she splintered apart, her mind going black as her body convulsed around his.

Garon wanted to watch her climax but her body was so tight, so hot and perfect that he couldn't hold back his own orgasm. The only thing he could do was hold onto her, helping her to make it better.

Layla felt his weight collapse on top of her and she would have sworn that this was the most incredible moment of her life. Every cell in her body was tingling, feeling more alive than she'd ever felt before.

"Layla," he said with that voice that sent shivers throughout her whole body. He lifted himself off of her and she instantly missed his weight but he pulled her against him so she was curled up next to his heat.

"Why?" she whispered when she could form words once again.

Garon knew what she was asking. "Because I won't let you go," was all he said as he pulled her closer and started the whole process over again.

Chapter 6

"I can't leave," she gasped when she stepped out of the shower, a towel wrapped around her.

Garon came out of his dressing room, pulling the knot of his tie into place. "That was exactly my intention," he teased, thinking she looked absolutely perfect just as she was. He didn't know of another woman who could look as perfect in a towel as his future wife.

Layla didn't seem to think her attire was appropriate though, nor was his comment very amusing. "My clothes!" She lifted her previously elegant silk blouse up, the tatters twirling in the air as she held it with her fingertips.

Garon glanced at the torn silk, then down at the remnants of her lace underwear. "I don't think that's the only item of your clothing that was damaged during that bout." He lifted the shredded lace up into the air and chuckled before stuffing them into his pocket.

She watched him for perhaps three seconds, not sure why he'd just done that. But when he didn't offer a solution to her problem, she huffed with a prickly temper. "You have to get me some new clothes," she told him, looking up at him with imploring eyes.

Garon put his hands on her waist, not letting her pull away this time. He was irritated that she was even doing that but suspected that it was only habit now. A habit he was going to break her of as soon as they said their vows, even if he had to keep her in bed for the entire two weeks they were on their honeymoon so she could get used to his touch and being close to him.

"I'll personally get you some clothes," he told her, kissing her forehead, struck by how much smaller she felt when she wasn't wearing her heels. She was a tiny, little thing!

Layla was horrified by that suggestion and grabbed his arm just as he tried to turn away from her. "You can't! There's no way you can be seen going into my bedroom!"

He chuckled. "Layla, you do realize that people are expecting us to be intimate, right?"

She glared up at him. "Only after the wedding!" she snapped, irritated that he was taking this so lightly.

"Would you like to borrow one of my shirts?" he offered.

Layla blushed, thinking that was not really an option. She could just see him watching her walk around in one of his giant shirts – and nothing else. "No. You might like that too much," she replied and shifted nervously on her bare feet. She was still clutching the knot of the towel over her breasts, desperate to keep what little cover she had when in this man's presence.

He had to agree with her. His eyes looked down at the towel she was still clutching, his fingers tugging gently just to tease her. "I certainly like this little ensemble you have going here just as much." Of course, if the towel were to come off, he wouldn't be upset by that in any way.

She rolled her eyes and smacked his hand away from her towel. "Could you please take this seriously? What am I going to do?"

Garon actually had no idea. There were so many people in the palace for the wedding, he wasn't even sure which rooms were occupied and which were filled. "Why don't you just call your mother…?"

She gasped in dismay at that idea, her free hand slicing through the air. "Not an option. My mother disapproves of me enough as it is. I wasn't born male, so therefore, I was immediately a failure." She looked up at him, worry coming into her eyes. "Please tell me you won't feel that way about…"

He stopped her quickly. "All children born of our union will be deeply loved."

She sighed with relief. It had been one of the things she'd meant to talk to him about before this moment but things…like him touching her or kissing her…kept getting in the way.

He took one of her shoulders in each of his hands, trying to reassure her. He'd gotten her into this mess by tearing her clothes, he should make sure he got her back to her suite with a minimum of embarrassment. "I'll have someone get me a blouse and I'll make sure it is delivered to you."

"Who?" she asked, not sure there was anyone in the palace she could trust not to gossip about this afternoon. It was too mortifying, knowing that some people had probably seen her being toted down the hallway. She could already imagine the stories that were flying through the kitchens and the housekeeping areas about their ruler's afternoon behavior.

"I'll have my guards do it. Will that work? They're the epitome of discretion."

She looked up at him, wondering what they'd had to be discrete about in the past. "Will they need to…" she stopped, not wanting to know the answer.

Garon waited for her to finish but she just shook her head. "Never mind."

Garon opened the door and said something softly to the guard standing outside. The guard immediately nodded his head, then quickly said something into his radio.

"It will be here in a few minutes," he told her after closing the door.

"You don't need to stay here with me," she told him, looking at him warily as he started to come back across the expanse of floor between them.

"You're standing in my bedroom wrapped only in a towel and you think I'm going to walk away?" He laughed as he shook his head. "I don't think I'm strong enough to do that. Not after the hours we just spent in that bed."

She grimaced. "It wasn't hours." She looked down at her watch and noticed the time. "Oh my goodness!" she gasped, her hand coming up to almost smack her forehead. "It was hours! How could you have done this?"

Layla hurried over to the doorway where her slacks and shoes were laying. Thankfully, she hadn't worn stockings or they would have been shredded as well. But since she'd worn slacks instead of a skirt, she'd left the stockings off today, not wanting to wear the horrible torture devices. She'd decided a long time ago, much to her mother's chagrin, that she would only wear skirts or dresses when she had public appearances. But since she obeyed all of her mother's very strict fashion rules during those public appearances, Layla was left to wear what she liked during the indoor or non-public times.

Garon's cell phone rang at that moment so she was saved from whatever he had planned as he spoke in French to whoever was on the phone. She hated to admit it, but she really loved listening to him speak in different languages. It added a different sort of essence to his authority.

In a very short period of time, there was a knock on the door and Garon walked to it and, a few moments later, came back to her. She stepped back automatically even while she was reaching for the blouse but he pulled it back, wrapping his arms around her and kissing her.

"I'll see you later tonight for dinner," he told her and finally handed her the blouse. "And don't think I didn't notice that you could have gotten all of your other clothes on while we waited for the blouse to arrive," he commented as he walked back towards the door. "You just wanted to torture me and that's okay. Because I intend to reciprocate the favor on our wedding night." And with that he walked out of the suite.

Layla stood there, the silk dangling from her fingers for several moments while the impact of his words hit her. It suddenly occurred to her that she wasn't as opposed to his form of 'torture' as she might have been this morning.

Then she shook her head, trying to dispel the silly magic spell he'd woven around her. She still didn't like him. She refused to fall in love with him. And this whole wedding and marriage thing was all just a convenience for him. She was just an appropriate female.

With her head back on straight, she quickly dressed and walked out of the suite, wishing there was a back way out. But she held her head up high and walked back towards the fitting room. She was just about to enter the sewing room when she remembered that several hours had passed and she turned around, not completely sure what was next on the agenda.

Chapter 7

The next thirty-six hours went by faster than she'd thought possible. They had their final dinner that night and Layla sat next to Garon, trying to ignore him as she focused all of her energy on his cabinet members, trying to put them at ease. And she refused to even acknowledge Garon's grumpiness, not sure what he had to be upset about.

The morning of her wedding, the sun was shining and the streets were filled with people eager to cheer on the royal bride and groom. She dressed carefully in her gold and ivory wedding gown, amazed that the veil didn't slip off because of all the hairspray the stylist used.

By mid-morning, she was a married woman. Garon took her hand and she lifted her head for the traditional wedding kiss. When she looked up at him, he literally took her breath away. She had avoided looking at him during the ceremony, afraid of what she might say or do. After yesterday, she knew more about this man than she wanted to know, more about herself as well, and she was actually terrified of their wedding night tonight. She'd gotten so out of control yesterday afternoon. As she thought back to those moments, she couldn't contain the blush every time. She'd been wanton! What had happened to all of her lessons on decorum? They'd certainly gone out the window as soon as he'd touched her like that.

So when he took her hand to lead her through the crowd, she only allowed her fingertips to touch his sleeve. Touching is what had started the insanity yesterday afternoon. Well, and her throwing a challenge in his face which she now understood was like waving a red flag in front of a bull. She certainly wouldn't do that again!

Garon didn't seem to mind her fingertips only approach. In fact, he seemed to be chuckling about it, or something else. She was too anxious to even ask him.

They posed for the official pictures, the family pictures, went through the motions of greeting their guests. When they finally sat down for the wedding meal, she couldn't believe how many courses were set down in front of her. She couldn't eat much of any of them, her stomach in knots as she anticipated the night ahead of her. She kept glancing out the window to where a large clock tower ticked down the time when Garon would take her away from all of this.

What made the whole thing worse was that everyone here, every guest as well as all of the people out on the street, would know exactly what he was going to do with her tonight. It was one thing when a normal person got married. Sure, everyone would know what was going on. But an entire country wouldn't be speculating about their evening's activities. Good grief, the entire world would be contemplating what they were going to do.

And she would not, absolutely would not, let herself get out of control again tonight! It was the mantra she kept telling herself as the tenth course was placed in front of her. That was not who she was! She was a lady! She was dignified and reserved. She had been chosen for this role because she was elegant and intelligent. Layla refused to be that crazy person who had appeared out of nowhere yesterday afternoon in Garon's bedroom.

Garon could feel the tension that was quickly rising inside of her. The tension in her shoulders and the stiff way she was sitting made him think that she was going to snap if she didn't relax somewhat. "What's wrong, my love?" he asked, bending down and whispering in her ear.

His lips brushed against the shell of her ear and she shivered at the unexpected touch. "Nothing is wrong, Your Highness," she replied and lowered her head so that the other guests wouldn't see her cheeks turn the silly, inelegant shade of pink.

Garon chuckled at her reaction as well as her feeble attempt to hide it from him. "After today," he started to say, lifting her hand and kissing her fingers, "I don't want you to wear so much makeup. I like seeing your cheeks burn from my touch, my lady."

She took a deep breath but looked out into the crowd of guests happily partaking of the wedding feast. She couldn't look at him and it angered her that they'd been married for less than three hours and already he was giving her commands. "I'll wear however much makeup is appropriate for the circumstances and event."

"Ah, we're back to that, are we?" he asked, lifting her hand once again and nibbling on her fingertips. He was anticipating her reaction and wouldn't let her snatch her hand away.

"Back to what?" she asked, turning her head and smiling to someone who waved to her as if they were old friends. She had absolutely no idea who the person was, but all the guests here today were either family members or representatives from the world's countries. This was not simply a marriage. This was a political union and everyone who was important wanted to be seen at this wedding. Not only was this marriage uniting two families but it was also helping to maintain peace between the four countries that had been at war.

Three men were approaching from the right and Garon stiffened for a moment, then she felt him relax once again. She looked in that direction, not sure who could get that kind of a reaction from her now-husband. But as she turned and let her eyes focus, she realized the importance of the next few minutes.

The three incredibly tall men approaching were all extremely handsome in different ways. Only one of them had a woman by his side and Layla was charmed by the adorable child in the man's arms. Man and child looked too much alike for her to mistake their relationship. And this man was incredibly proud of his son.

The four men greeted each other as if they were old friends when, in reality, they had been enemies only a few months ago. This camaraderie was a welcome relief and everyone in the room had stopped to observe the greetings, eager to see how this meeting progressed. The importance of their words could not be under represented. These four men controlled a huge portion of the oil in the world, not to mention, had an enormous influence on world economics. So their friendship was a welcome relief to observers from around the world and would be reported in news analysis for the next few weeks.

"Looks like I was too slow," Sheik Dassar bin Sarook of Altair commented as he turned to greet Layla. He bowed over her hand, kissing her fingertips with polished gallantry.

Layla smiled at the man, startled that she didn't feel the same thing when this man kissed her fingers as she did when Garon executed the same caress. "It is indeed a pleasure to meet you as well, Your Highness."

He winked down at her, trying to ease her nerves at such an ominously watched greeting and Layla was both enchanted by the man's insight as well as relieved that he was making the effort to put her at ease. "We are all excited to have your help in maintaining this peace. I know with a beauty like you on his arm, he will be too distracted to notice that I'm going to win the oil contracts next month."

The three other men laughed and Layla smiled up at the man. "And I will enjoy the challenge of focusing him on his responsibilities," she replied, subtly telling Garon that she wouldn't become his distraction.

The men laughed even harder, even Garon chuckling at her not so subtle jab. "She loves me," he told the men, all of whom started punching Garon on the back in their manly way. Layla turned to the only other woman in their group. "You must be Calliendra," she said, taking the woman's hand.

"Please call me Callie," she replied back, taking Layla's hands in both of hers. "And if you need any advice on how to handle these kinds of unbearably arrogant, insufferable, infuriating men, please don't hesitate to call me. I know what you're going through," she said with a knowing look at her husband. Layla wanted to laugh when the man simply raised one of those handsome, dark eyebrows in her direction. The little boy in his arms tried to mimic his father, but he couldn't raise just one brow so both of them went up although he did the you'll-pay-for-that expression extremely well.

Callie noticed Layla's startled expression and she glanced over her shoulder at her two males. Turning back to Layla she said, "Oh, just ignore them. They always think they're right. It is our job to show them the truth."

Garon looked back to the man and the boy, then all the men moved a bit closer, trying to intimidate the beautiful blond woman but she simply looked right back at all of them. Layla was fascinated when the men backed down but her husband simply rolled his eyes and pushed her ahead. "You will have no contact with Her Highness," he told his wife.

Callie only laughed and, before she was pushed out of the way, said quickly to Layla, "I'll call you after your honeymoon!" and then they were gone, lost in the crowd.

Dassar moved up and took Layla's hand next. "You are lovely and I'm jealous that this old man found you first," he said and kissed her hand regally. "We will soon have much to discuss."

Layla had no idea what he meant by that statement, but she smiled politely. She was stunned yet again when the last of the men stepped forward. "If he ever treats you poorly, just come to me and I'll…"

He didn't have a chance to finish that statement since Garon growled at the man. Layla knew that he was only teasing and she took the man's hand again. "I appreciate your concern. I know that it isn't misplaced."

With that, the handsome man threw back his head and laughed, delighted as he moved on as well.

Garon put his hand around her waist and pulled her against his side. "You've made a couple of new conquests, my lady."

Layla's heart felt lighter after that encounter. "Those are your former enemies?" she asked, just trying to clarify because they all seemed like extremely charming men.

"Former enemies," he confirmed. "They are friends now. Friends I deeply respect and admire."

Layla looked over to where the three men, woman and child stood, all of them talking and laughing about something and she was jealous that she couldn't join them. They looked like a group of people she could relax and enjoy spending time with.

"I can see why," she told Garon. She was looking forward to getting to know the blond. Callie seemed like she could be a wonderful friend when Layla had thought not to have any alliances. She'd anticipated facing a lonely existence as she learned to navigate through the politics of both marriage and administration issues but the idea of being able to confide in a good friend as well as someone also in her position, someone who knew what she was going through, made her feel…relieved. Happier!

"We have more people to greet, my lady," he said and turned Layla back to the other wedding guests.

Layla knew that it had been an honor bestowed on those leaders to be the first in line to greet the wedding couple. But looking out into the enormous number of guests, she wasn't sure how she was going to get through the rest of them.

"We don't need to speak with everyone," Garon told her softly, obviously reading her mind. "There are just a few important people we should speak with before we can leave."

Layla heard those words and the prospect of greeting each and every person in this room seemed to be not such a bad idea. At least while she was here with the guests, she wasn't liable to throw herself into Garon's arms. And her clothes wouldn't be torn apart. She blushed, thinking about how she'd had to walk back to her rooms without underwear yesterday afternoon.

"Come, my lady," he said. "Let's get this over with so we can be alone."

Layla bit her lower lip, but she moved forward with Garon. One by one, she stood beside him as he introduced her to the various dignitaries and his family members. She'd met most of them over the years, but he was introducing her to them as his wife. It was all symbolic and she might have laughed at the whole situation if she weren't so terrified of losing herself in Garon's arms again.

On one side, she supposed it was a good thing that she was sexually attracted to her husband. Her life could be so much worse. Her arranged marriage could have been to a disgusting, smelly, gross man with a long, weird beard and a gut that would make it difficult for him to walk.

Looking up at Garon, she had to admit that he was shockingly handsome and he treated her kindly and respectfully. At least when they were in front of others. It was only when they were alone that he....

She shivered and Garon, so attuned to everything about her, looked down, his eyes silently questioning her. She shook her head slightly and forced herself to smile. He squeezed her hand even as he turned back to the prime minister.

She had less than an hour of introductions before Garon started making noises that they were to leave the celebration. Layla's stomach tightened. She knew what was going to happen! This was it! Garon would take her out of this reception and....

"What's wrong?" he asked, bending lower so that no one else could hear their conversation.

Layla looked up at him, realizing that he was shielding her from the rest of the guests with his body and she appreciated his kindness. "Nothing is wrong," she told him, lying even though her trembling increased and she knew that he could feel it.

"You're nervous again, aren't you?"

She bit her lip and shook her head. "I'm fine," she replied.

He sighed, blowing the wisps of hair off of her forehead. "And even our activities yesterday can't ease your fears of what is to come." He wasn't asking. He could feel it in the way her body was stiff and unyielding.

"I'm fine, Garon," she said, trying to be stoic even when faced with more humiliation at his hands.

He pulled her closer. "You're not fine."

She decided to give him part of her concerns. "You're going to take me out of here in a few minutes, aren't you?"

"Yes," he replied. No quibbling about that response.

"Everyone here, the entire country, will know what you are planning, what we're going to be doing." Her eyes were lowered but when he just stood there, not saying a word, she looked up at him.

He was smiling! The rat was laughing at her.

With a huff, she almost reached up and smacked his arm but she restrained herself. It wouldn't do for the guests from around the world to see her smacking her new husband. That definitely wouldn't look good on the tabloids of the world. She could just imagine women all around the world standing in line at the grocery store and laughing at how she'd punched her husband on her wedding day. "You're right," she said with as much dignity as she could muster and trying very hard not to follow through on that punching instinct. "I'm being silly. Let's just get this over with."

She was turning to head for the exit, more than ready to do walk out of this reception all on her own. Maybe others might think she was just exiting for a slight break in the celebrations if she could....

Garon realized what she was going to do and pulled her back to his side, not letting her go even when she struggled. "I'm sorry," he told her, his lips very close to her ear. "I wasn't laughing at you, Layla. I was just surprised at what you were worried about. I thought you were concerned about what was going to happen. Not the fact that everyone here knows it is going to happen."

She was once again surprised at how astute he was. "Well, that too," she replied, trying to be honest with him since he was so perfectly on track.

His hand slid around her waist more securely and she felt his thumb gently rubbing against the fabric of her dress. Even through the beadwork and layers of fabric, that touch still sent excitement racing through her body.

"So yesterday didn't help? You're still afraid of what is going to happen?"

She looked away from him. "Yesterday actually made things worse." She looked around, her eyes glancing everywhere but at him.

She felt his hand grip hers and her eyes darted back up to his. "How could yesterday make things worse? Explain." Then he raised his hand, stopping her from speaking. "No. This is not a conversation we are going to have in the middle of five hundred people." With that, he placed her hand on his arm and led her out of the reception.

Layla lowered her head when the cheers and clapping started and she tried to pretend that she was somewhere other than here. She wasn't walking through a ballroom packed with strangers, family and friends to a private room where this man is going to do wicked things to her. No, this simply wasn't happening.

She was actually walking down a pathway to a tropical island. She pictured the warm sun on her shoulders, the stone pathway, the wind rustling the palm fronds overhead…

"Are you still with me?" Garon said as they stepped out of the room.

She sighed, the tropical island dissipating in her head. "Yes," she replied back with as confident a voice as possible. Unfortunately, it came out only as a whisper. When she looked up though, she found that they were no longer surrounded by all of their wedding guests. The only people in the hallway with them were the guards that always surrounded Garon.

And her shivering became even more intense. He felt that instantly and tightened his hold on her hand. When they reached his private quarters, he pulled her inside and closed the doors before turning to face her.

"Okay, talk to me," he said, dropping her hand and moving deeper into the suite. He stopped in front of a bar and poured two glasses of something that looked delicious but she wasn't exactly sure what it was. Handing one to her, he took a stiff sip of his own glass.

Layla watched in fascination as he divested himself of the formal, stiff jacket, tossing it over one of the chairs in the sitting room, unconcerned about all of the metals and ribbons that jangled with the callous treatment. He was still wearing a tailored shirt but that extra fine cotton stretched over his extremely broad shoulders, making her feel small and more than a little defenseless.

"Layla, if you continue to look at me like that, there will be no talking. At least not for a long time."

She jerked out of her thoughts of his shoulders and looked up at him, caught the heated expression in his eyes and shuddered. She took a sip of the liquid in the glass, then coughed. "What is this?" she asked, trying to catch her breath as the fire from the liquid burned her throat.

"Brandy. I was hoping you might be more relaxed after a drink."

She shook her head and set the glass down on the table nearest her. "Not working," she choked out.

"Hell," he mumbled and a moment later, he moved closer to her, taking her into his arms. His hands framed her face as he lowered his head, intending only to kiss her, to feel her lips against his and try, somehow, to reassure her that things would be okay. Better than okay, he thought.

But then she moved her lips under his and he lost control. The need to possess her overwhelmed him and he couldn't hold back. Her whimper of need and the way her hands slid up the front of his chest added to that urgency. And also the realization that this was his wife. This was his woman. She was finally his. He had only known her for a few days, but it didn't matter. He wanted her, she was his and she was in his arms. He had to have her.

Lifting her up, he carried her into his bedroom. When he was there, he lowered her legs and slowly, with as much reverence as he could, unwrapped this beautiful woman that was his wife from her wedding finery. That crazy possessiveness removed all thoughts from his mind except for the need to please her, to drive her just as crazy with need as he felt.

Layla tried to think. She tried to remain cool and passive in this activity. But he was kissing her with a reverence and passion that was spinning her out of her mind. She had no idea how it had happened, but suddenly, she was standing in front of him naked except for her bra and underwear. And her high heeled shoes.

And where on earth had his shirt gone? She didn't care! Her fingers were now free to touch and explore. She realized she hadn't done much of that yesterday, too shocked and crazed to do much more than react when he'd touched her. But now! Now she could touch and explore! She leaned her head forward, unable to stop her lips from pressing a kiss against the middle of his chest. There was an indentation at the bottom of his sternum that was just fascinating to her. She ran her finger over the indentation, back and forth, unaware that Garon was loosening the pins in her hair. Her hands moved off to the sides while her mouth moved in for another kiss and her fingers accidentally moved over the flat, male nipple. When that happened, she heard him hiss air through his teeth so she tried it again and got the same reaction.

It was addictive, she realized, making him moan or hiss. She moved her hands everywhere, searching for more places that would cause him to make a sound. The best was when her hands moved lower over his rippled stomach, following the interesting line of dark hair that disappeared below the waistband of his slacks.

Garon waited, his hands still as he wondered what she would do. When her fingers hesitated, he couldn't hold off any longer. His hands moved quickly, dispensing with his slacks and his boxers, standing in front of her naked. "Now what?" he asked, hoping and praying that she would continue.

She looked up at him, her face pink with both embarrassment as well as fascination. "I can't…"

"You can," he told her and he took her hand, ignoring the way she tried to pull back. He wrapped her hand and fingers around his erection, closing his eyes at how good it felt. "Layla," he whispered.

And because she liked the way he said her name so much, and couldn't believe how interesting that part of him felt, she continued to touch him, running her fingers tentatively over the shaft, feeling all of him. Her fingertips explored the skin, amazed at how hard it actually felt.

"Layla!" he grumbled, louder this time but she ignored him. She ignored the odd sensations low in her belly that were tightening in that weird way that they'd done the previous afternoon. She ignored the heat emanating from him and all of her thoughts that were telling her that a lady wouldn't do something like this. She knelt down in front of him and she ignored the cursing from above, too intent on exploring this part of Garon, this forbidden part that she wanted to understand.

Her fingers still touched and explored and when she wrapped her fingers around him, there were guttural, ferocious sounds from his chest. She realized that his hands were fisted in her hair but she didn't care. All she wanted was to...did she dare? Could she really do it? She looked at his male member, her heart beating so hard, so fast. And she dared! She wanted so badly to do this so she leaned closer, her tongue darting out and quickly retreating.

Glancing up at him, she was afraid of his reaction but she couldn't see his face because he had his head thrown back and his jaw was clenching. "Am I doing it wrong?"

Garon couldn't believe her words. He couldn't believe she was able to speak because he wasn't sure if he was able to respond. But he saw the worried look in her eyes and he pulled up every ounce of control he could and shook his head. "Layla, I guarantee that you're doing it exactly right. In fact, I don't think there is a wrong way."

He tried to loosen the curls from his fist, afraid he might be hurting her scalp but then her mouth closed over the tip and he roared with the pleasure of her wet, hot mouth on his male member.

He shook his head and lifted her up, unable to endure her tentative ministrations any longer. "I can't take any more of it, Layla," he growled as he lifted her into his arms and laid her on his bed. He couldn't even take the time to look at her, needing to touch her, explore her just as she'd done to him. He wanted to show her what she'd done to him in the most basic way.

Holding her hands over her head, he kissed her, his tongue mating with hers until she was moving underneath him. When he felt her respond, he moved to her neck, nibbling his way down her body. He released the front closure of her bra but couldn't take the time to remove it, too intent on kissing and touching those perfect mounds. When she screamed out, he moved to her other nipple, biting, nipping and sucking until she screamed and tried to pull away from him. He laughed, a deep sexy sound when she tried to offer her breast back to him. He quickly took the offering, making her scream and move and only when she tried to pull away did he release that prize.

Moving lower, he nibbled at the soft, sensitive flesh of her stomach, then moved lower. She tried to close her legs but his big body was already between them and he wasn't allowing her to hide from him in any way.

When he moved lower, he felt her try to pull her hands away. He let go of her wrists but only so that he could do this part of his woman justice. When he felt her hands in his hair, he ignored her tugs as well as her cries of "No!" and just had his way.

When his tongue darted against her thigh, he almost laughed with the joy of how responsive she was. She jerked and tried to scoot higher, but he had hold of her hips and held her down, pulling her right back to his mouth where he licked and teased his way to his goal.

When he pulled that sensitive bud into his mouth, he heard her scream as she lifted her hips up, almost offering him her body. He might have laughed, but he was too intent on making her scream out again so he slipped one finger inside of her, then two, all the while, moving around, teasing, tasting, sucking. When the scream came again, he could feel her body explode around his fingers and his mouth and he thought it was possibly the most erotic thing he'd ever seen in his life.

Moving back up, he positioned himself right at her entrance but he waited, wanting to see her eyes as he entered her for the first time as husband and wife. When her eyes finally fluttered open and he saw the sensual smile on her beautiful mouth, he almost groaned with need but still he held back.

"Look at me Layla," he commanded. She sighed and looked up into his eyes, and he moved slowly into her heat, gritting his teeth because she felt so incredibly good. "You're mine," he told her even while his mouth was still kissing her and his body was fighting to hold back so that he could pleasure her one more time. "Put your hands on me, Layla."

She arched against him while her hands moved up to his shoulders. As he pushed into her heat, she felt him pressing, stretching her. She waited for the pain but it wasn't there this time. It was only intense pleasure as he filled her up, making her feel more complete than she ever had in her life.

Her hands moved down from his shoulders to his chest and she ran her fingers through that dark hair, loving the way he felt against her. When he was fully inside of her, she pulled her knees up around his hips, taking him even deeper into her body and she gasped at how perfect, how full and amazing it felt.

He shifted until he was right where he wanted to be, her body wrapped around him, her legs around his waist and her hands on his shoulders and arms. He didn't move for a long moment, savoring this time, this intense pleasure at just being a part of her. "Now you're going to release all that control again. You're going to fall apart in my arms and you're going to continue to scream out for me."

She shook her head, unaware that she'd already done that only moments before. "No," she whispered but then he moved and the denial came out as a gasp. And oh, he knew how to move. The man was a virtuoso and played her body perfectly. Moving inside of her, shifting and adjusting, causing the most glorious friction she'd ever imagined. What he didn't know was that she was already lost, she was so lost in his movements that she couldn't think, couldn't hold back. So when he picked up the pace, she threw back her head, arching into his pounding while she screamed out his name, digging her nails into his arms as her body splintered apart.

Garon held out as long as he could, but she just felt too incredible and he couldn't hold back his own climax any longer. Holding her in his arms, he rode the wave of incredible pleasure.

"You're beautiful," he said as he rolled over, pulling her onto his chest.

Layla rubbed her cheek against his chest, wondering what had just come over her. She didn't like the woman that she became when he touched her. She hadn't liked it from the first moment he'd held her hand.

"Why?" she whispered. It was the same question she'd asked yesterday as he was holding her in their aftermath but this was a different question.

"Because you were meant to be right here, in my arms. You're the perfect lover," he told her, skimming his hands along the curve of her back. "And I like it when you can't hold back from me."

She buried her face in his warm skin, wishing she hadn't been so crazed. "I don't like it at all."

He rolled again, this time so that she was underneath him and he could see those fairy eyes of hers. "Why not?"

"I don't like losing control. I don't like being out of control in any situation."

"Even in bed?"

"Especially in bed!" she snapped, wanting to scoot out from underneath him but he just slipped his leg between hers, trapping her more completely.

"Explain," he commanded, his hands still even though he wanted to touch her, feel her come alive under his fingers and mouth once more.

She shook her head. "Can I please just get up?" she asked, fighting tears. "I need to take a shower."

"No. You're going to talk to me. You've been resisting me ever since we met. I want to understand why."

She blinked hard, trying to stifle the tears that threatened. She knew from the look on his face that there was no way she could say anything other than the whole truth.

"You have your world, Garon. You have power and control over the things in your life. Perhaps not everything. But you have more than most people." She blinked back the tears and looked over his enormous shoulder, unable to make eye contact with him when revealing something so personal to him. "I have no power. I was sold to you. My father's representative and yours haggled over my price." She looked at him then, wanting him to understand how that felt. Her blue eyes glared into his darker ones, begging him to understand. "Put yourself in my place and think of how I feel. You might have had to get married, Garon, but at least you had a choice. You might have been given three or four candidates and you got to choose which one suited you the best." She let those words sink in for a moment. "I didn't have any choice. I woke up one morning and, over a meal, my father announced that the negotiations were finalized and I was to marry you." She blinked again, her fingers curling up into fists so that she couldn't touch his tempting chest any longer. "I hadn't even been told that marriage to you was a possibility."

She could tell that he didn't completely get her perspective. "I want some control, Garon. I have nothing else except my physical body and you take even that away from me. And so I don't like it. I don't like losing control, but I have no choice when you touch me."

He loved those words even if he didn't like the way she was saying them.

"I'm not so bad for a husband, am I?" he asked, easing his hold on her wrists. He shifted so that he was almost cradling her now. Because she had a valid point. He'd never understood her resistance but her words, as well as the tears she was fighting to control, were tearing him apart.

"I'm sure that, when I get over my anger and resentment towards my life, I will find you a very acceptable husband. And you probably didn't have much say in who your wife was either."

Garon didn't mention the hundreds of photos and biographies he'd gone through. He'd narrowed the selection down to ten woman and his aides had done the rest of the work. "Would it help if I told you that I'm thrilled with you as my wife? More than thrilled? I consider myself a very lucky man."

She laughed, but it sounded a bit like a hiccup. "The sex is good for you."

He rolled his eyes. "Layla, if you're going to try and tell me that you didn't enjoy what we just did, then I'm going to have to prove you wrong and do it all over again. And I'll have more focus this time."

She did laugh at that comment, but she buried her face in his chest while she laughed. "Please don't," she gasped. "I don't think I could take any more."

"Then you're willing to acknowledge that the sex was good for you too?"

She sighed, resting her chin on his muscular chest. His head was propped up by a pillow behind him and he was looking down into her eyes with a challenging look.

"Yes, you obnoxious man. I'll acknowledge that. If you'll admit that you wouldn't like to be powerless."

He looked at the curls of her hair that were now splayed across his chest and her shoulders. She looked beautiful and he understood. "Yes. I can see your point."

She'd never thought that acceptance or understanding would make her feel significantly better because she would still be trapped, still be in the same predicament. But she had to admit that his words of understanding meant a great deal to her. And in a strange way, they did help. "I was raised to become some powerful man's wife," she explained. "I was taught how to entertain without causing offense, to charm angry dinner guests, to maneuver around a party with ease. I know what to wear to any occasion, how to do my hair, my makeup, how to smile so as not to cause offense to anyone while at the same time, not be overly effusive either. I had no choice in my future. I wasn't given the option of becoming a scientist or a librarian. I was told that I would become a wife. A wife without power."

He shifted once more, his lips kissing her neck. "Ah, but you forget that I was raised in that manner as well. There was never a choice for me. I was taught from an early age to recognize lies, to manipulate events to benefit my country, to see through what someone was telling me and know that they were basically trying to manipulate me." He kissed her ear, biting the lobe. "I was raised to know who to sit next to, who to avoid." He moved lower, his hands caressing her breasts, noting that her breathing ratcheted up as his fingers teased her nipples. "I was never allowed to show weakness because I represented my country. Showing weakness in any way meant that my people were weak, my country's defenses were weak."

She loved the way he was touching her and his words started to ease something inside of her. He had a valid point as well. He hadn't had many choices either. He understood what she was going through.

She didn't have a chance to tell him that because he was moving further down her body. "Garon, what are you…" she gasped when she felt his fingers down along her thigh. "You don't have to do that," she whispered, but her whole body was tense, waiting for him to do just that. And when his mouth did, she couldn't hold back the noises his activities caused. And for the first time since she'd met this man, she felt free. She felt like something had broken through and she didn't try to stop those sensations from screaming through her body as she shouted out her release. Garon understood! She was reveling in that realization as well as her climax when he moved up her body and filled her up, rolling her over so that she was on top this time.

"And now you are in charge," he told her, taking her hips and showing her what to do.

Layla bit her lip as she concentrated on this new position. "I'm in charge," she whispered, smiling as she moved against him, thrilling in the way he let her move and shift, finding her own rhythm that she enjoyed. In the end, Garon wouldn't give her complete control. He rolled back over and finished them off but Layla didn't mind. She actually preferred this side of Garon. And it made a huge difference in how she viewed their marriage after talking with him.

Chapter 8

Fourteen days later, Layla sat in the council room, listening to a group of men debating the various issues. Layla didn't know why she was sitting here. It was a complete farce that she should sit through the council meetings. The men sat at the table, arguing back and forth about the proposals bandied about on the issue of military reforms, environmental controls, immigration policy, even the more recent border problems.

She stifled a sigh as each of the men went through their arguments again, trying to convince the others that they had the better idea. Layla looked over at Garon, her mouth falling open slightly when she realized that he was staring right back at her. The man wasn't paying any attention to the topic under discussion. In fact, he looked like he was...

He wasn't!

He couldn't be!

Good grief, the man was making love to her with his eyes!

Her body turned hot, then cold, then she had to shift uncomfortably in her chair when he slid his finger over his lower lip. It was as if he were sending her a message that he wanted to kiss her, to bite her lip. When his eyes dropped to her breasts, she looked away. She was already feeling that strange sensation in her belly, which she knew from experience now what he could make happen. But Layla wasn't going to encourage him in this distraction.

She focused all of her attention on the man speaking, refusing to look at Garon. Unfortunately, she had spent two weeks alone with him and she knew what he was thinking. She knew the exact moment that his eyes shifted lower, then back up to her eyes. She could feel the heat from his gaze, knew exactly what he was doing and where he was looking.

She was not going to look at him, she told herself. He could stare at her all he wanted but she would not be pulled into that mental game.

No!

She shifted again in her chair, still refusing to look at him but she could feel his gaze.

Sure enough, when her eyes were pulled back to his, he was staring at her. Hard! His roguish eyes were telling her that he would not let her get away with even silent disobedience and her whole body tightened at the sinful promise. Her mouth fell open and she squirmed again despite all of her efforts to remain aloof and reserved. When his lips twitched up into a knowing grin, she sighed and rolled her eyes. Not enough so that anyone else could see but enough so that he got her silent message.

A message that he ignored.

"No, we're not going down that road," he interrupted his council, proving that he was the master of multi-tasking. All the time that he had been making love to her with his eyes, he'd been paying attention to the fervent arguments going on around him.

She almost resented him for that ability. But in the end, she had to admire him for his proficiency at concentrating so well, even when he was obviously thinking about two different issues. He really was a brilliant man.

The conversation moved on and there seemed to be no end to the number of issues that needed to be discussed. But there was one subject in particular that caught her attention. Someone mentioned building a road through the mountain area. She sat up straighter in her chair, trying to listen more attentively. That mountain contained several villages that would be destroyed if the road went through in the direction they were proposing. She'd visited those villages only last year. They weren't wealthy towns and the people came and went through the mountains easily whenever they needed to get something from their neighbors, but building the road would devastate their way of life.

She listened intently, trying to hear about the other possibilities. There was another option, she thought. If they could just build the road around the mountain instead of through it, that would save those people and preserve their way of life. The people of that village might live a subsistence existence, but they preferred it that way. They wanted it that way. When one of the villagers wanted a different way of life, they moved on although she knew that many of them came back when they grew tired of the frantic way of life outside of their village.

She had been told how the whole town would pull together to help someone if they wanted to leave, to find a different way of life. And each of the villagers had relatives so they knew exactly what they were missing. This was not a poverty-stricken village. This was a group of people who banded together to live a subsistence existence because they chose to do that, wanted to appreciate life and the earth and sky. They knew what was out there in the big, bad world and they'd decided to live in the mountains in order to avoid that.

"Why would we blast our way through the mountains," one of Garon's advisors argued. "It is cheaper to go around the mountain. And safer as well."

Layla relaxed when that argument was offered. It made sense and several of the others were already nodding their heads about the issue. She relaxed back against her chair, feeling relieved that the issue might be swayed away from the mountain road. But when the vote was cast, it was split right down the middle with only Garon not voting.

Layla tensed but she couldn't think of any way in which to sway his vote. She didn't want that road to be built directly through the mountain, but who was she? She was only his wife, a little woman who he probably didn't think knew enough about the issue to voice an opinion.

Her anger started to simmer and she clenched the arms of her chair.

"We'll table this issue until after lunch," Garon ordered and quickly stood up, walking out of the council room.

Layla jumped up from her chair and moved off towards the dining room herself, frustrated that she felt so powerless in this situation. She'd love to just walk up to Garon and tell him to vote one way or the other, but that wasn't her role and she doubted that Garon would appreciate her stepping into his responsibilities. She didn't want to eat with these men, she thought. And especially not Garon.

"Layla," Garon called out, his long legs easily catching up with her.

He took her arm and guided her out of the main dining room and towards the area reserved just for the two of them. "Apparently we have something to discuss."

Layla couldn't stop the glare in her eyes but she smothered her anger, tamping it down deep inside of her. This was not her role, she told herself yet again. Garon didn't want her opinion, just her company and….

It was no use. She couldn't stop the anger from welling up inside of her at the idea of those men, probably this man standing in front of her, plowing through a small town's village simply because of expediency. It was just wrong! She followed him, but as soon as they were seated and their lunch was set down in front of them, he nodded to the servants to leave them alone.

He poured her a glass of white wine, then lifted his own glass. "Okay, tell me what's wrong," he started off.

Layla looked at him carefully and then decided to simply present her arguments to him and he could be angry with her. She simply couldn't be quiet about this village. It was wrong and he had to know it. Someone had to stand up for the people who didn't always have a voice, she rationalized. So instead of swallowing her resentment, Layla passionately defended the rights of the mountain people to not have their way of life disrupted simply because it will cut a half hour out of a person's drive around the mountain area of the country.

Garon didn't interrupt her until the end of lunch, nodding his head at each of her points. When he lifted his linen napkin to his mouth and stood up, he simply said, "Okay."

Layla stood up as well, not sure what he meant. "What do you mean, 'okay'?" she demanded, assuming she'd failed in her efforts to protect that quaint mountain village. She was ready to lambast him for being so insensitive and ignoring all common sense when it came to defending his people. But the look in his eyes caused her to hesitate for a moment.

Garon took her hand and led her back to the council room. "I mean, okay, I won't let them build the road through the mountain."

She stopped and that forced him to stop in the middle of the hallway. "Just like that?" She stared up at him, stunned for a long moment as her whole body waited for clarification.

Garon shrugged one of those massive shoulders. "Yes. You presented a good argument," he told her, tugging her hand so that she would start walking again.

Layla walked, but her mind was spinning. He agreed with her? Before lunch, he'd seemed undecided but now he was agreeing with her? Could it really be that simple?

He escorted her over to her chair before resuming his own seat at the head of the council table. All of the other advisors were already in place and everyone took their seats when Garon sat down. "We'll go around the mountain," he announced. He turned to the man in charge of the transportation department and went over the details, giving additional guidance about the road situation. After that, the next subject was brought up and no arguments were made against Garon's decision.

Layla sat in her chair, her mind still in a whirl. He'd agreed with her! She'd stated her opinion, told him why the villager's choice in how they lived was important and he'd accepted her argument! She'd offered her side of the debate and he'd accepted her opinion.

Looking at her new husband, she couldn't believe that he'd done that! She felt…empowered for the first time in her life.

She felt her cheeks start to warm when she thought of the few other times he'd let her take charge. Every once in a while, when she was very firm and gave him that smile that told him she wasn't taking no for an answer, he'd let her take charge in bed. And he only gave her that control for limited amounts of time before he took that control back. Goodness, she liked it when he allowed her to have her wicked way with his body, touching him everywhere that she wanted. It was never long enough though. She didn't realize that her eyes were unfocused and her mouth had opened slightly as she remembered those secret, private moments in their bed. Of course, he didn't give her full control, and he generally took charge of their lovemaking again quickly. It was pretty easy for him to do that too, with his superior strength but he was always gentle and careful as he expertly reversed their positions on the bed. And then he emphasized his power by lifting her arms over her head and driving her insane with desire but she was okay with that aspect of their lives. Now more than ever.

Something blossomed inside of her and she relaxed back against the chair, her eyes never leaving Garon's handsome face as she contemplated the end of this council session. Layla wasn't sure what this new feeling was about, but she felt all tingly and warm inside.

Chapter 9

Two days later, Layla stood outside in the heat, feeling miserable but there wasn't anything that would convince her to go inside. She stood stiffly, her hands clasped together in front of her and tried to ignore the trembling.

Garon walked out of the palace, his eyes watching Layla carefully. "Are you okay?" he asked.

She nodded her head, her fingers clenching together tightly. "I'm fine," she replied, lying through her teeth. "Have a safe trip," she told him finally, not wanting him to leave without those words.

Actually, she wanted to beg him not to go, not to leave her. She had been in this man's company almost constantly for almost three weeks and, the sad truth was, she was going to miss him! She'd never thought she would feel like this. If anyone had told her a month ago that she would be fighting back tears simply because her husband was going on a three-day trip, she would have laughed at the silly notion.

She had to remind herself that this was a political union. An arranged marriage. Garon needed a wife and an heir to maintain the peace after the horrible war, to give his people a belief that they had a secure future.

He didn't need to hear about this strange, desolate sensation she was experiencing at the thought of him not being close. She didn't want him to know that she probably wouldn't sleep in their bed tonight, because the thought of not being wrapped up in his arms made her want to scream out. She wouldn't be able to sleep in that huge bed without him. She'd already mentally decided to sleep on the sofa in their sitting room.

Garon looked down at her, noticed the trembling in her full lips and the way she was fiercely blinking back tears. "Is there anything you want to tell me?" he asked, taking her hands and pulling them apart so he could hold them in his own.

Layla's eyes shot up to his. Did he know? How could he know? She'd kept her secret so well hidden from him!

Or was he just testing her? Was he probing? And he really didn't know?

She opened her mouth to tell him, not sure exactly how to say the words. But in the end, she didn't have the courage. She'd just realized her secret herself and she wasn't sure how she felt about it.

Being in love wasn't the amazing emotion others seemed to think of it, she thought as she looked back down at their hands. She was gripping his tightly and tried to loosen her hold, but he wouldn't let her.

She started to say something again but the only thing that came out was, "Hurry back, okay?" she whispered, her eyes glued to his blue tie because she was afraid her feelings for this man would be shining through in her eyes. Good grief, wouldn't that be the ultimate humiliation?

Garon wished that she would tell him about the pregnancy. She'd been sick the past few days and hadn't been eating well until late in the afternoon. But looking at her now, her face so sad and the dark circles under her eyes, he wondered if perhaps she wasn't aware of it. But if that were the issue, why was she looking so sad?

Damn, he loved this woman. And he had no idea how to get her to fall in love with him. He hated that they'd started their relationship out as a political union. With every cell in his body, he wished that they'd met somewhere and fallen in love naturally.

But he understood her side of the issue. She'd been forced by her family and circumstances into this marriage and she was holding back her feelings. Would she ever release that aspect of their lives and would she allow herself to fall in love with him?

He pulled her into his arms, unconcerned with the guards looking on. He wanted to kiss his wife goodbye and he was going to do it. Even though he was only going to be gone for three days, he was still going to miss her smiles and those fairy, blue eyes that he loved looking at when she woke up each morning.

And her laughter! Damn, she was a light that broke through the tedium of his days. He hadn't even realized he was looking forward to them until she hadn't been in their suite one night. He'd been furious and demanding to know where she was. And when he'd found her, when she'd directed that sunshine-bright smile in his direction, he finally accepted that he was madly in love with his wife.

"I'll try and cut the trip short," he told her. "There's only so much the other guys can talk about, right?" he said and she was the only one who could hear his words. His guards knew about these quarterly meetings at the Fortress of the Guards but the rest of the world had to remain out of the loop. This was the time when the four leaders got together to talk about anything suspicious that might be going on, discover any faction that might be trying to disturb the peace between the four previously-warring countries.

She laughed softly, amazed and comforted that he would even suggest such a thing. "This is important," she told him, placing her hands on his chest. "Go be brilliant."

He bit her earlobe and loved the way she wiggled against him. But in the end, she pushed him back, encouraging him to leave.

Layla's heart was beating wildly as she watched him walk towards the armored cars that would take him away from her. She was always amazed at how kind and gentle he was with her, how he loved to touch her and make her squirm but as soon as he stepped away from her, it was almost as if he pulled a cloak over his shoulders. When he was with her, he was just a man. A gorgeous, sexy, confident man who made love to her until her toes curled with desire. But when he stepped away from her, he was a ruler. He was hard and commanding. His entire body language changed, became tougher, more demanding and authoritative.

She had to admit it was a fascinating transformation.

But then he stepped into the car and his bodyguard closed the door. She could no longer see him but she still stood there, wanting...needing, to be as close to him as she could for as long as possible. Even now, she could feel the sparkling electricity of his presence even though he was behind a bulletproof door.

The long caravan of SUVs pulled away from the palace and headed towards the protective gates where officers had stopped traffic several blocks way so that the caravan could leave the palace with a minimum of risk. She didn't move until the car turned the corner and she could no longer see his vehicle. Layla sighed, her shoulders sagging dejectedly as she slowly walked back towards the palace that would no longer be exciting now that Garon was gone.

She'd almost made it inside the palace doors when she heard an explosion. Everyone around her ducked in reaction and she looked back down the road. The explosion was outside of the palace walls....

Exactly where Garon's convoy had gone!

For long, painful moments, she just stared, the acrid smoke billowing upwards. In fact, everyone stared, their eyes riveted on the ball of flames going up in the air. When the smell hit her, the metallic scent permeating the area, it seemed that the scent was the trigger that got everyone to jerk out of their surprise.

Suddenly, people were running everywhere, chaos reigned for several moments until the guards' discipline kicked into overdrive. The chaos turned to men forming a perimeter, radios stopped the chatter and moved into crisis information only.

Layla was the only one that couldn't seem to move, wasn't sure what was happening. All she knew was that the man she loved, the man she'd only recently learned to love, was either hurt or...no, she couldn't even think of the possibility of Garon not being alive. He had to be alive. Her heart simply couldn't function without Garon in her life.

That thought, the possibility of Garon being hurt or trapped or…spurred her into action. The guards had already started their procedures but she didn't care. Her only thought was to get to him, to see him and make sure that he wasn't….

"Garon!" she screamed and started running towards the ball of fire. Someone stopped her, she had no idea who but she clawed and scraped at the arm holding her back, trying to get free from the person who was keeping her away from the man she loved with all of her heart and her mind and her body. She had to get to Garon! She had to save him! "Let me go!" she screamed, clawing and kicking. "He might be hurt! I have to get to him!"

Her bodyguard ignored her commands. Instead of releasing her, he bent down and slung her over his shoulder, carrying her into the palace and into safety. He ignored the way she was pounding against his chest, taking the beating because his only priority was to get her inside the palace walls and to safety. She was now surrounded by guards, all of them with their weapons drawn and her mind was almost crazy with the need to get to Garon, to make sure he was safe.

"Put me down! I have to find Garon!" she screeched frantically. But they weren't letting her go and a moment later, she covered her mouth, trying to stave off the nausea. "Bathroom!" she gasped, her eyes wide with the very real possibility that she might get sick right here in the foyer of the palace.

The man holding her around her waist whisked her up into his arms and carried her to the bathroom where he locked her inside.

Layla rushed to the toilet and threw up, her body wracked by the pain. When she was somewhat presentable, she banged on the door, needing to get out and find her husband. "Please! I'm fine now. I just need to get to him. I need to make sure he is okay." She was sagging against the wooden door, her fingers clenching desperately against the doorknob that was the only way she could stay upright as the fear for her husband, the man she loved so desperately, raced through her mind. Images of previous bombs flashed through her mind and she was almost sick again just thinking about her husband in pain. It couldn't be, she told herself. He was too strong, too stubborn to let anything as silly as a bomb hurt him.

Wasn't he? Oh, please, she prayed, let him be too strong and too stubborn! Let him be impervious to the shards of metal and chemicals that could so easily tear a vulnerable body to shreds with so little effort.

The guard opened the door, concerned that she might hurt herself if she continued to bang on the door, but he wouldn't let her out. "Your Highness, we can't let you go outside the palace."

She clutched at the guards arms, unaware of the tears streaking down her cheeks or that her hair was no longer perfectly in place. "But Garon!" she cried. "He's out there! What's happening? Why aren't all of you out there finding him?"

The man listened on his radio even while he held her back, knowing that she would run out of the palace if he released his hold on her waist even slightly. There was a lot of chatter but he remained holding onto her, not letting her go for any reason. He nodded as he listened, then turned to face her again.

Turning to the queen, he grabbed her by her shoulders with each of his hands and bent lower so that he could see into her eyes. "He's fine, Your Highness! He's fine." When she stopped trying to pull his hands away from her shoulders and listened to him, she stared up at the man, still trying to absorb his words.

"He's fine, Your Highness," he stated again, this time in a calming voice. "The missile hit one of the other vehicles but it is armored. The driver and guards have some minor burns but they are okay."

Layla heard the words and nodded her head. She knew she should be concerned about the other guards, but all she heard was that Garon was okay. And then there was nothing. Blackness overwhelmed her and she felt herself falling without any way to stop that fall.

Chapter 10

Garon pushed the doctor away, his need to see Layla and make sure that she was okay overriding all of his decisions right now. Another doctor kept trying to rub something smelly on his burns but he only wanted to see Layla. He'd been told she was okay, but he wasn't believing any of it until he saw for himself.

When he walked back into the palace, he looked around, thinking she should be right there in the foyer but his eyes scanned all of the people that were rushing about, not seeing his wife. His anxiety rose several levels, thinking that someone had gotten to her while all the guards were out reacting to the explosion.

"She fainted, Your Highness," one of his bodyguards told Garon, already getting the information and relaying it as quickly as possible. They all knew that information was the key to getting control of any kind of a situation like this so the radio was an open line of continuous chatter in a very specific process.

Garon almost sprinted down the hallway. When he reached the open doors of their private suite, his eyes searched frantically for his wife. When he finally saw her, lying on their bed, her face white and her body lifeless, he couldn't believe his eyes.

"Layla," he whispered, hurrying to her side. He took her hand, feeling how cold it felt and tried to rub life back into it. "Is she going to be okay?" he demanded of the doctor.

"Yes, Your Highness. She just fainted," the doctor assured him.

Garon stared at his wife's pale features, his heart pounding with fear for this woman. "She's pregnant," he told the doctor.

He'd been about to inject her with something but with Garon's statement, he pulled the needle back. "Are you sure?" he asked.

"Pretty sure," he said, not taking his eyes away from her while his hands tried to rub some life into her body, to infuse her with some of his strength.

The doctor put the top back on the syringe and pulled out something else. The foul smell permeated the room but a moment later, Layla was pushing the man's hand away, her stunning blue eyes coming back into focus.

"Layla!" Garon growled and almost shoved the doctor out of the way so that he could pull his wife into his arms. "Damn it woman! Don't do that to me!"

Layla shivered as Garon's arms enfolded her, giving her much needed warmth. "You're okay," she sighed and then she started crying. "You're okay!" she sobbed, getting his chest wet with her tears.

The rest of the world faded away as he rocked her gently back and forth. For several long moments, they stayed just like that, neither of them willing to release the other as their minds took in the reality that the other was okay, had survived this horrible morning.

As his muscular body held hers, her mind slowly absorbed the reality that this man was okay and that she hadn't lost him. There would be one more day when she could feel his arms around her, to revel in his strength and the amazing man that he was. Goodness, she loved him so much it actually hurt. Unfortunately, the rest of the world also snuck into her consciousness. She knew what he had to do, what the world needed to see and hear. "You have to go on television," she said, but she didn't loosen her arms from around his neck.

"I know."

"Everyone will need to see you, to be sure that you're okay."

He actually tightened his hold. "I know."

With one more breath, she held him close. But she knew what needed to happen. She knew that she had to release him so that he could reassure his people. "Go," she said and she pulled her arms away. "You need to do this. Just go, okay?"

Garon lifted his hand, his thumb rubbing the remaining tears from her cheeks. "Are you sure you're okay?" he asked.

"Yes," she told him and forced a smile. "I'll get cleaned up and I'll be by your side in a few minutes. They'll want to see me as well," she told him.

He nodded his head and looked out the window. There was still the smoke as the fire fighters worked to put out the flames of the exploded SUV without damaging any of the evidence his security team would need to find out who did this.

"What a mess," he said but he stood up. Layla was right. His people needed to see him, to see both of them. He needed to get out there and show them that the terrorists hadn't won.

As he walked away, she watched his body language change yet again. Gone was the tender lover and in his place was the strong, commanding ruler who would assure his people that he was fine and their future, their country was also fine.

From that moment forward, there was so much to do, so much to investigate. The police and palace guards were everywhere, gathering evidence, speaking with witnesses. Reporters were out on the street filming and Garon, with a bullet proof vest underneath his suit, was directing the police, giving them information and basically just showing the world that he wasn't hurt, nor was he even concerned about another attack.

By the end of the day, there were still no leads as to what had happened or why someone had bombed Garon's motorcade, but all evidence was pointing towards a resurgence of hostilities between one of the other countries. Garon refused to believe it. The head of the military was called in and ordered not to retaliate. He argued, but Garon gave him a direct order and he agreed to obey.

"But, Your Highness," the gruff, elderly man said, his uniform stiff and ready for battle. The man was the perfect person for the role of head of the military because he knew strategy as well as comprehended the impact of communal psychology on a nation during a war. But in this instance, Garon wouldn't allow him to think along the lines of retaliation.

"Something doesn't smell right," he told the older man.

Layla watched all of this with growing trepidation. Garon had spent hours gathering evidence. She was angry with the person who had done this and she was furious with herself for feeling angry. She was even angry at Garon for putting himself in danger. But throughout the day and evening, she hid her feelings, knowing that Garon had to focus on the evidence and not on her. He needed to deal with the situation logically and having to reinforce her would only slow down the process.

"Are you ready to prepare for dinner, Your Highness?" Layla's maid asked from the doorway of the secured room where his advisors and lead military personnel were gathered as they all discussed the findings.

Layla glanced at her watch, shocked to find that it was already time for dinner. She'd skipped lunch, not even aware of the passing of time as she went through one interview after another, checking in with Garon after each one. She'd just needed to see him, to verify with her own eyes that he was still okay.

Unfortunately, she wasn't hungry. She opened her mouth to tell her maid that she didn't want to have dinner. But she stopped, thinking about her mother's words. Routine, schedules. Rituals must be adhered to. People expect them. They need them. The palace staff was just as scared about the morning's events as everyone in the country but they weren't privy to the information being tossed around inside this room. They were all going about their duties, scared and confused.

She needed to show them that things hadn't changed. The business of the palace would continue. Layla had no idea how she was going to swallow food, but she would do it so that everyone would see that she wasn't going to let this get in the way of her life. It wouldn't slow her down, so it couldn't slow them down either.

So in the end, she nodded her head and walked to their suite to dress for dinner. It would be expected, she thought with an ache in her chest. Not just the crowds outside, but the palace staff would need the routine, they would need to know that nothing has changed.

She pulled on an evening gown and let her maid pull her hair up into some sort of style. She had no idea what she looked like or even why the maid was trying so hard, but she sat through it all, wishing that she could find Garon and hold him close, forget the rest of the world. Someone had just tried to kill her husband! And she was having her hair done.

Her mother would be proud!

She walked with her head held high and her shoulders back, all the way down the hallway to the main dining room. People were coming in and out, Garon was dressed in a suit, cleaned up from the afternoon, but every part of him was all ruler now. He was their sheik. He was the man they were all turning to for answers.

But he was her husband!

Garon was just about to walk into another meeting with his military leaders, ready to hear options. But he turned and looked at her as she headed into the dining room. Instantly, he knew that she was not okay. Walking over to her, he took her into his arms and Layla felt horrible. He was the one that had been attacked today. Not because he was a bad person or because he'd hurt another human being. He'd been attacked only because he was the ruler of this beautiful country. Someone had tried to hurt him because of what he was and not who he was.

She lifted her hand and smoothed his tie, thinking that she'd done almost the exact same thing earlier this morning. "Are you okay?" she asked.

He looked down at her with amusement in his eyes. "I'm more than okay now that you are here."

She laughed. Sort of.

"Let's have some dinner," he told her.

Layla pulled out of his arms. "You were going into another meeting," she told him, looking at him with a wry expression in her eyes.

"Yes, but I need to eat."

"And the palace staff need to see you eat."

His eyes widened at that comment. He'd been so concerned with reassuring the crowds outside of the palace that he hadn't thought about the cooks, chefs, maids and all of his administrative staff who were also affected, shaken and worried. "You're right," he replied, squeezing her hands to tell her how much her comment made sense. "Thanks for thinking of them as well."

He turned to his chief of staff who was standing several feet behind him. "Tell everyone to take a break and have some dinner. The chefs probably already have everything ready to go, they're just waiting for someone to enjoy their efforts."

The man quickly nodded his head, agreeing that a break was a good idea. Bowing, he stepped backwards, going into the room where the next meeting was to take place so that he could announce the break himself.

Garon turned to Layla. "That was very thoughtful of you."

"Everyone needs to eat. And full bellies make better decisions. I'm sure everyone's blood sugar is pretty low right now, hyped up on caffeine."

He chuckled. "You're right. Jumpy minds don't make wise decisions." He took her hand and led her into their private dining room. "Tell me about the interviews. What is the feeling of the people based on the questions the reporters are asking you?"

And as the servants brought in one course after another, they discussed their day. While most people around the world were talking about soccer practice or piano lessons, she and her husband evaluated their success at reassuring their people that their ruler had not been assassinated.

Chapter 11

Layla stepped into their suite, pulling her earrings off and setting them carefully on the dresser. She'd been here so little time that she hadn't had a chance to redecorate but, as she stripped off her shoes and stockings, pulled the pins out of her hair, she focused every cell of her brain on how she would change this room. It was her attempt to not think about how close she'd come to losing the man she…

No. She wasn't going to think about that any more. It was over. Time to move on.

It was late. Or early, perhaps. She wasn't really sure what time it was any longer. She suspected that it was in the early hours of the morning and she should probably be tired. But she wasn't. She was still wired by everything that had happened.

"Talk to me, Layla," Garon said standing behind her.

She looked at him in the mirror, her mind still on the kind of dressing table she'd like to put in here. "We might need a smaller bed," she told him, putting her diamond earrings on top of the ornate, wooden box that held his cufflinks.

Garon sensed that she was in a strange mood, but he wasn't sure what to do about it or what to say. She looked exhausted, but in a wired, hyped up way. "Okay. We'll get a smaller bed. What are you thinking?"

She carefully worked the clasp on her diamond bracelet, her fingernail slipping underneath the hook closure. "I'm thinking…" she pulled too hard and broke a nail. "I'm thinking that I hate jewelry!" she yelled, wanting to rip the bracelet off of her wrist.

"Let me get that for you," Garon said, moving forward.

"No!" she came right back. Her eyes were wild as she dared him to approach her. "Don't bother! I can do this myself!"

Garon wasn't sure what was going on. "Layla, talk to me, love. Tell me what's really making you angry."

Layla swiped at the tear that fell, shaking her head. "Nothing! I'm not angry at all! Everything is perfectly fine I just can't get this stupid bracelet off." And with that, she walked into the bathroom and slammed the door.

Layla stared at her reflection in the mirror, not sure what was happening to her. All she knew was that her body hurt. Everywhere. She leaned against the countertop but as the tears started flowing and the sobs wracked her body, her legs could no longer hold her upright. She let her back slide down the cabinets, her whole body curling up into a heap as the fear reverberated back and forth from her mind to her heart. She wasn't sure which hurt more and, at this point, she didn't care. All she knew was that she wanted this pain, this soul-rending fear, to go away.

A knock sounded on the door and she jerked upright. "Layla, are you okay?"

She wiped her face and stood up, using the counter to hold her up. She took a band and pulled her hair back then quickly started washing her face. "I'm fine," she called back, not giving him any details. Talking through the door helped to mask the strange tone of her voice.

Garon was not fooled though. "You're not okay. I can hear it in your voice."

Layla ignored him, not wanting to talk with him tonight. Or ever, she thought.

She finished washing her face and walked out, grabbing a pillow off of the bed and walking out of the bedroom.

Garon saw the pillow in her hand and the intent in her eyes. Fury welled up inside of him. "What the hell do you think you're doing?" Garon demanded, noting that she was still in her evening gown.

Layla ignored him as she walked over to the sofa. She plopped the pillow down and started to do the same but Garon grabbed her arm and spun her around. "Layla, so help me if you don't start talking to me…" He let the threat hang in the air between them.

She jerked her arm out of his grip and laid down, ignoring him when he towered over her.

With a muttered curse, Garon stomped back to the bedroom, obviously furious but unwilling to try and get her to talk about whatever was bothering her. He suspected she was still upset about the attack, which would make sense, but if she wasn't going to talk to him, he couldn't help her. And he was damned if he was going to beg.

Layla lay on the sofa, images of the explosion and ball of fire, not to mention Garon's face, covered in black soot after the horrible attack, running through her mind. Over and over, she pictured the day, the events of the morning frame by frame and she couldn't stop the trembling or the tears. But she kept her pain silent, not wanting Garon to storm back in here and try and talk to her. She was finished. She wasn't going to do this any longer. She knew he needed an heir, but he'd just have to find some other woman to produce that child with because she couldn't do this.

This love, the painful, wrenching fear of losing him, wasn't going to work for her. She couldn't do it. She'd just discovered her feelings for him and then this happened. It wasn't fair and she just…nope. She wasn't going to deal with it. She couldn't. She wasn't strong enough.

Garon lay on the bed, staring up at the ceiling as his anger increased. He could hear her sniffling in the other room and he hated the sound. When he heard her hiccup, he knew that she was crying and he couldn't take it any longer. Her sobs made his chest and his gut ache. Not to mention, he wanted her in his arms where she belonged.

Snapping the sheets back, he walked into the sitting room and stared down at her. She was curled up into a ball of misery on the sofa, the blanket barely covering her as she sobbed out the pain and confusion she was feeling. She still wouldn't look at him so he took matters into his own hands. Literally.

Lifting her up, he carried her into the bedroom.

Layla had known that he was beside her but she couldn't look at him, couldn't see his magnificent body that was most likely naked because the man didn't own a pair of pajamas. Why would he? Why cover up anything as magnificent as that body?

But she hadn't been expecting him to simply lift her into his arms. "What are you doing?!" she demanded, trying to get out of his arms but he was too strong and he held her wiggling body easily. "I'm not sleeping with you!" she raged, too afraid of what she might reveal to him if she fell into his arms again.

"You're not doing a hell of a lot of sleeping out there either, so you'll just have to be miserable in here. With me!"

Layla jumped up the moment he put her into bed. She was still in her evening gown but as she stood up on the other side of the bed, she looked at him and gasped. "You're naked!" Damn it, she'd known he would be but the sight of him standing there still had the power to make her body tingle all over. She knew what this man could do to her, how his simple touch could make her body arch and beg and plead for more.

Garon rolled his eyes. "Of course I am! I was in bed. Right were you should have been!"

"Put some clothes on!"

"Get into bed, Layla," he commanded through gritted teeth.

"No! I'm not getting into bed with you."

He was exhausted from hours of meetings and briefings, bruised from the attack and hard as a rock because she was close by. He wasn't going to put up with this any longer. "Get into the bed, or I will make you!"

Layla stepped back, her anger going up another ten notches. "I'm not getting into bed with you!" she told him, pointing at the messed up bed. "I'm not having sex with you. I'm not having a child with you. I'm not falling in love with you and I refuse to be married to you any longer."

"Sorry, but all of those things are already happening. There's not a hell of a lot you can do about it!"

She inhaled sharply. "Want to bet on that?" she shouted back, her hands fisting at her sides while she put the bed between them.

Garon suddenly understood what was going on and his anger instantly evaporated. His eyes softened even if his body couldn't. "You're angry about this morning, aren't you love?" he asked with a calmer voice.

She stiffened, fearing that he could see into her thoughts so easily. "This morning only proved that I am not the woman for this job. You'll just have to find someone else."

And that was the crux of the issue, he realized. Walking around, he approached her carefully. "Layla, today was wrong. But it won't happen again."

She watched him, backed up until she was cornered but still shook her head. "No Garon! Stay away from me. And don't make promises you can't keep."

She was right. He couldn't promise that there wouldn't be another attack. "Okay, so let's go through your issues," he suggested. "First of all, you're already married to me. So, at least for the moment, that isn't going to change."

"I'll change it quickly," she told him, wiping at the traitorous tears that fell down her cheeks again. Why couldn't she turn off the water works, she asked herself? It was horrible the way she was angry one moment and tearful the next. She should be stronger but she couldn't seem to stop the roller coaster her emotions seemed to be on today.

He didn't argue that point but there was no way in hell he was going to let her divorce him.

"Okay, then let's look at the other issues. You're not going to fall in love with me."

"Right!" She nodded her head for emphasis.

"But honey, you're already in love with me." He watched her fairy eyes widen and he tried hard not to laugh. "And I love you."

She shook her head. "No! This is an arranged marriage. Love has nothing to do with what we have."

He shrugged his shoulders. "I love you," he repeated. "And you love me. It shows in the small things."

She sobbed and covered her mouth with her hands. "No. I refuse to love you." She knew that she was madly in love with him, but she didn't want to admit it out loud. That would make it more real, more powerful.

He took her shoulders gently, pulling her closer. "You love me. And I love you to distraction, so let's just go over the other issues."

He picked her back up in his arms and carried her over to one of the big chairs, sitting down with her in his lap. "So we're in love with each other and in an arranged marriage. Seems like things worked out pretty well."

"Except someone is trying to kill you," she cried, unable to hold herself away from him any longer. Her arms wrapped around his neck in a vice-like grip but Garon didn't mind. He'd rather not breathe than to have her leave him. Rubbing his hands up and down her back in a soothing manner, he addressed her issue. "Someone is always trying to kill me. I get death threats daily."

Her arms tightened around him with those words. "Make them stop," she sobbed.

He laughed softly. "We'll tighten security around the palace and I won't leave for a while. At least until the threats are less credible. Okay?"

She thought about that for a moment. "Okay," she sighed, weak with relief that he was at least taking the threats seriously and would take precautions.

"And you're already pregnant with our child, Layla."

He felt her whole body stiffen with those words. She pulled back to look at him, her blue eyes wide and unfocused. "I'm not pregnant."

He looked down at her. "Are you sure? You're sick every morning and feeling fine in the afternoon." He waited a moment before he continued. "We've been together for three weeks and you haven't had your period. Are you telling me that you had it right before the wedding?"

Layla's body just about blacked out again as she counted back the weeks. She should have had her period more than a week ago! "I'm not pregnant!" she whispered urgently.

He touched her lips with his thumb. "I think you are."

When her mind finally accepted the possibility, the sobs only increased. She wasn't sure what to do or to think. "I can't divorce you if I'm pregnant."

He laughed as she sagged against him. "I wouldn't let you divorce me even if you weren't pregnant, Layla. You're my wife. We're in this together."

She shook her head. "No. I'm not strong enough for this. I can't handle it."

"You can. You did." He leaned back, coaxing her to relax against his chest. "And you handled everything beautifully today. You were right there, ready to help with whatever came up. You soothed the excitement right along with me and I'll never forget that. Every reporter was charmed and the palace staff think you're some sort of goddess now. They love you and I suspect most of them would die to protect you."

She buried her nose against his throat, having trouble swallowing because she still hadn't been able to face the reality of what someone had tried to do earlier today. To him! They'd tried to kill her husband! "I was so scared. I thought I'd lost you."

"I didn't die. I wasn't even hurt."

"You could have."

"Yes," he replied, accepting the truth. "It is always possible that someone could kill me. But I employ a large number of very intelligent men and women who are all dedicated to preserving my life," he said that with a bit of derision. "They are dedicated to their jobs and are still looking to find the person who did this." He let his words sink in before he continued. "I don't know about you, but I'd rather spend as many days with you as possible rather than live without you somewhere else."

She didn't move as her mind absorbed those words. "What are you saying?" she asked.

"I'm saying that I love you, Layla. And I know there are risks but even a normal couple could walk out the door and one of them could get hit by a bus. But we don't live by those fears. We move on. We live life and we," he covered her stomach with his hand, "raise our children to be strong and help to mitigate these problems."

Her hand moved to cover his where it lay on her stomach, her breath catching as she thought about the possibility of her carrying his child. "You really think I'm pregnant?" she whispered, thinking the words were scary enough.

But then it hit her. A child! Garon's child! Goodness, she couldn't believe the hope that a potential pregnancy generated within her. "Pregnant," she whispered the word reverently.

"Would you be upset?" he asked, watching her carefully. Was she one of those women who didn't want to have children? He didn't think so, but she didn't appear to be jumping for joy right at the moment.

But her next words reassured him. "No. It would be thrilling. I would love to have your children," she told him.

He turned his hand over so that he was holding hers.

"We'll get through this," he told her, reassuring her with a gentle hug. "But you're going to have to admit that you love me."

She trembled at his words, not sure what she could say to that. "I don't..." he stopped her words with a kiss.

"I don't want to hear lies, Layla," he told her. His fingers tangled in her hair and he pulled her head around so that those strange, blue eyes were looking directly at him. "Tell me," he demanded.

"No," she whispered.

He chuckled and kissed the side of her mouth. "Tell me," he coaxed again.

"I can't," she told him, moving closer to him.

"You can say the words because you know that you do." He nibbled on the side of her neck, smiling to himself when she shivered. "Layla, the sun is going to be coming up very soon and we need at least a few hours of sleep before the day starts again. I'm going to make love to you as soon as you tell me what I want to hear, so hurry up so we can get some sleep."

She shivered but shook her head. "If I say it…"

He pulled back. "No. You won't be giving me any power over you, Layla. I love you. Totally, completely and unequivocally. That isn't going to change. I love you and I'm going to spend my life making you happy. And you feel the same way. So just admit it and we can move on to more interesting things," he nibbled on her lower lip. "Like getting you out of this dress so you are as naked as I am."

When he did those things to her, she couldn't hold back. It had been like this from the first time they'd met and she wasn't sure how to fight it. Furthermore, she wasn't sure she wanted to any longer. Fighting him was too hard. And it would be such a relief to actually admit it and just deal with the consequences.

"I love you," she finally admitted.

Garon stilled at her words. And then his body went into overdrive! "I love you too," he told her with so much feeling. He lifted her into his arms. Standing her next to the bed, he quickly divested her of all clothing and then, with minimal effort, he gently laid her on the bed. "I love you, Layla," he told her again as he kissed her.

Layla's tears streamed down her cheeks once more. Never in her life had she cried as much as she had in the past few weeks.

"Why the tears?" he asked as he lifted one onto his thumb.

Layla sniffed. "Because you're right."

He chuckled as he slid his body over hers. "What was I right about this time?" he asked, nuzzling her neck.

She laughed despite her tears. "I don't think I can tell you."

He laughed but his teeth gently nibbled at the end of her long finger. "Fair enough. Will you tell me that you love me again?"

"I love you. And you're right, that admitting it doesn't make me feel weaker." She smiled when he nuzzled her breast, her hands catching his head. "It makes me feel much stronger."

He stilled with those words. "You're beautiful, Layla. And I swear I'll love you so much, you won't know what hit you!"

She laughed at that. But he began his lovemaking in earnest after that so there wasn't much more laughter. Only a great deal of sighing, begging and pleading until he took her so high, she swore she was catching the stars in her hands.

Afterwards, he held her in his arms, not allowing her any space. "I love you," she whispered only moments before she fell asleep, content for the first time in a long, long time.

Epilogue

"I love him," Layla grumbled as she moved slowly down the long hallway of the ancient fortress. "But if he doesn't stop worrying about me, I'm going to kill him."

Callie laughed as she waddled next to her new friend. "I know what you mean. Last night, I had to get up to go to the bathroom. The moment I moved towards the edge of the bed, Zahir was awake and carrying me in his arms to the bathroom."

Layla shook her head. "I guess some women would think that's pretty sweet," she said. She wasn't one of them, she silently thought.

Callie growled low. "He wouldn't leave me until I was finished. He's afraid I'll slip on the bathroom floor!"

Layla's hand came up to stifle her laughter.

"Sit down!" Garon called out.

Layla and Callie spun around, both of them glaring at the man who had yelled the order. Callie's eyes shifted to her husband's though. He was the bigger threat at the moment since he was walking towards her with a determined stride. She held out her hands to stop him but he kept on coming. "Don't you dare pick me up, Zahir!" she ordered to him.

The man didn't even pause with that threat. He didn't stop until he'd reached his wife, towering over her. "Sit down or I will carry you over to one of the chairs, Callie!" he told her.

Callie turned to look at Layla. "See? This is what I have to deal with!" She then turned back to her husband. "I don't want to sit down. I want to move around and exercise. I am not going to gain fifty pounds during this pregnancy like I did with Luca!"

Zahir bent lower. "You'll look beautiful if you gain fifty pounds. You will not look so beautiful if I have to spank your adorable bottom because you fell or hurt yourself."

She poked him in the chest. "I'm pregnant! Not an invalid! I can walk around and I'm darn well going to do it."

Layla moved away from the two of them as they fought. Callie really did look huge. She was about six months pregnant and glowing. She was one of the most beautiful women she'd ever seen and Layla was impressed with the way she stood up to her enormous husband. Of course, Garon was about the same height and might even have a bit more muscle on his massive shoulders, and he no longer intimidated her either.

"You're not sitting down."

Layla spun around, having forgotten that he'd commanded her to sit. She laughed softly at his glare. "I thought you and the boys were going to show Luca how to play croquet.

Garon's eyes didn't leave her face. "We are. We're just setting up the wickets."

Layla peered around Garon's huge shoulders, her mouth falling open when she noticed where the adorable little boy was directing Terek and Dassar, two very powerful sheiks of the other countries, to put the wickets. "How in the world are you going to hit the ball up the side of the fortress wall?" she asked with exasperation. Her eyes followed the other wickets that had already been set up. "And on the stone pathway? Any balls hit over there will go on forever!"

Garon just shrugged his shoulders. "We'll be creative," was all he would say.

"You'll go nuts," she mumbled. "I'm going to sit over there in the shade. I'm only three months pregnant, Garon. Don't you dare try and treat me like a china doll. I won't stand for..." She couldn't finish her sentence because he'd simply lifted her into his arms and was striding across the field to where the two chairs had been set up in the shade, icy drinks already poured on the table in between. He deposited her in the chair and Layla turned to find Callie being carted over to the other chair.

"I guess we lost that argument," Callie grumbled as her husband and Garon both walked away, having gotten their way.

Layla sighed, but she couldn't pull her eyes away from the broad shoulders and tight butt of her husband. "I guess there are worse things in the world we could have to endure besides being coddled."

Callie was having the same problem with her own eyes. "I guess so. But I can't wait for the other two to bite the bullet and get married. It will be more fun if there are more than just the two of us. We might be able to gang up on them a bit more effectively."

Layla picked up her glass of freshly squeezed lemonade and nodded her head in agreement. "So which do you think is going to fall next?" she asked.

Callie watched the four men and her son start to play croquet. "I have no idea, but you're going to witness the most amazing cheating in the next hour or so. I'm just warning you now."

Layla and Callie had a wonderful time, laughing so hard at the men that they were bent over, holding their stomachs as they watched the men get the croquet balls through the strangely placed wickets. Luca, Callie's adorable son, was declared honorary mallet holder on most of the plays. But even Layla was impressed when Dassar picked Luca up and balanced him on his feet while Luca lifted the croquet ball on his knees and somehow got it through the wicket that had been set up on the wall.

The others were just as insane, the rules ignored, balls had to be replaced because the men would smack one another's' balls so hard that they'd be lost in various, unknown caves within the fortress.

But throughout the whole event, one thing rang clear. Layla was sure that none of these men were the ones who had tried to assassinate her husband.

So who had been the mastermind of the threat?

She had no idea. All she knew was that she loved these people, considered Callie almost a sister by the end of the long weekend, and Zahir, Dassar and Terek were wonderful leaders who would never resort to such underhanded tactics. What's more, the four men were genuine friends. Discussions over dinners that secret weekend centered around the border fights that had started to break out as well as the attempt on Garon's life.

Unfortunately, no clear answer could be discerned.

As Layla lay in Garon's arms, both of them exhausted from their recent lovemaking, she sent a silent prayer of thanksgiving that her husband had survived. And that he'd chosen her for his wife. Out of all the women he could have chosen, she knew that she'd ended up the lucky one.

Excerpt from The Sheik's Blackmailed Bride, Book 5 in The War, Love, and Harmony Series

Chapter 1

"Have you contacted Faris and put my proposal to her?" Sheik Dassar bin Sarook asked, his eyes snapping while he walked to his next meeting. Faris was his current mistress, a beautiful woman who would be an adequate wife. He wasn't sure about mother, but he could always hire someone to act as nanny after children were born.

Hasif, the sheik's harried chief advisor, hustled to keep up with his employer's longer stride. Hasif was shorter by a foot and severely overweight, but he was a brilliant man when it came to details, allowing Dassar to focus on the bigger picture for Altair. After the seemingly relentless ten-year war, there was so much to do in order to bring prosperity back to Altair, and Dassar was not going to make his people suffer any more than they had to. Already, the economy was starting to come back to life and people were becoming more secure in their future.

The peace treaty with his former adversaries was a good one and Dassar was determined to put the final requirements into place as quickly as possible. Marry and secure succession with an heir. That was the plan for all four of them and Dassar wanted to finalize that issue as quickly as possible so his people knew what to expect. He knew that both Zahir and Garon had found women that were both beautiful and generous of spirit. He didn't think he would be that lucky and just wanted to find a wife that would fulfill the role. Someone outside of Altair and the other three countries so that the possibility of war breaking out wouldn't happen again.

"If I might be so bold," Hasif put in, huffing a bit as they rounded the corner of the palace. "Perhaps there might be a better answer to the need than the lovely Faris." Hasif had to bite the side of his lip to keep himself from cringing as he said the next words about the most selfish woman he'd ever met in his life. "I know she would be eminently eligible for the role of your wife, but I'm just putting an idea out there that perhaps there might be a better solution."

Dassar stopped and looked down at his advisor, causing the man to almost run into him with the unexpected stop. "Better solution? Faris is beautiful and composed, exactly what Altair needs." And he wouldn't fall in love with her, he thought. Exactly what *he* needed for a queen.

Hasif took pains to keep his expression blank. Any sort of disagreement might push this hard and tough man to do the opposite. "I agree, Your Highness," he replied, treading carefully since they were speaking about the man's current mistress. But Dassar went through women like some men changed ties. It wasn't that he was promiscuous, although he certainly had a way with the ladies. Charm and harsh good looks, not to mention extreme wealth and absolute power in his country were potent aphrodisiacs. The women flocked to him. Just by raising his finger, women almost ran to him, eager to warm his bed.

Hasif would admit that the woman in question was indeed lovely, but Faris was also cold and self-centered. She was spiteful to the palace staff and more intent on spending as much of her lover's massive wealth as she possibly could. When she wasn't catering to Dassar's every need in the bedroom, she was barking orders at the palace staff, interfering with Altair policy and being one of the most demanding, rude, inconsiderate women Hasif had ever had the misfortune to endure. The only break from this treatment was when the woman flew in Dassar's personal jet to one of the clothing capitals of the world to spend his money.

Hasif had worked hard to come up with an alternative for Dassar's marriage problem, and he hoped he'd found a good solution.

"Although Faris is indeed lovely, I'm not sure that she would be accepted by your people with open arms." He said that carefully, not sure how close Dassar was to the woman. If history had repeated itself, the lovely and evil Faris should have been on her way out the door a month ago. Hasif suspected that the only reason Dassar hadn't grown bored with her was because of the mutual agreement with the other three countries for each of their leaders to marry quickly and produce that heir. Since two of those rulers were already happily married, the pressure was on to do the same in Altair.

Hasif suspected that Faris knew about the marriage requirement as well, which was why she was so confident about her current role. And also why she'd become extra demanding lately.

The woman was pure evil, Hasif thought. It was imperative that Dassar find a woman with a heart inside of her chest and not just a cash register. After all the years of war, all the sacrifices his ruler made in order to protect the interests of Altair, Dassar deserved someone who would love him with all of her heart. Hasif was of the opinion that Faris, no matter how lovely she might be, could only love herself and the things she could earn from her time in Dassar's bed. And Hasif seriously doubted that Faris would trouble herself to bear Dassar an heir. The woman would manipulate events so that her outstanding figure remained intact – not destroyed by the potential ravages of pregnancy and birth.

And so he'd come up with another option.

"Why do you think she won't be accepted?" Dassar demanded, irritated that the issue had not been resolved already. He had too many things to do with his time; worrying about his marriage was not something he wanted to waste any time on.

Again, Hasif chose his words carefully. "She might be a bit harsh until one gets to know her softer side," Hasif said carefully, not mentioning that there wasn't a softer side to that horrible woman. "But I have another option. I have a woman who might be a better fit for this role. Someone a bit more docile and who…"

"Who is she?" Dassar demanded. If Hasif was doubtful that Faris could fulfill the role of his queen, then there was a legitimate reason for caution and looking at other possible candidates.

Hasif handed Dassar a file. "Read through this information, Your Highness. I think that this woman might be a perfect option."

Dassar took the file but didn't open it. "Fine. I'll read through it later. What's going on with the refinery in the south?" he asked, moving again towards his next meeting. And just that quickly, his marriage was pushed aside so that he could concentrate on more important issues.

The next meeting was just as tedious as the previous one and Dassar grew impatient with the arguing over the oil revenue. "Enough!" he called out. He opened the file in front of him, thinking that it was the file that contained the list of options for the refinery. But instead, his eyes were captured by a set of startling blue eyes surrounded by a cloud of platinum-blond hair. The lighting caused the blond tresses to look almost white and sharpened the contrast to the blue eyes. Her skin was pale with rosy cheeks, bringing to mind the image of a soft, English rose with blush colors and a pale center.

His eyes skimmed through the information, quickly absorbing the details. Hasif had done an excellent job of gathering intel on the woman and Dassar couldn't deny that he was intrigued. His initial reaction was to reject the idea. This woman, Dassar looked at the top of the page for her name, this Luna Montgomery, was too soft, too tender. She'd never make it in this world. Altair was a beautiful country and in another ten years, he would ensure that it was peaceful and economically stable. But the war had destroyed a great deal of the country's infrastructure. It was a difficult life here and there was a great deal to rebuild. Palace politics and intrigue alone could do in the average woman with a sensitive heart.

This Luna woman was only twenty-four years old. Not old enough, he thought and flipped the page. Reading through the letter she'd sent, he shook his head. She was pleading with him for a six-month reprieve for her little town in Central Virginia. Apparently, the recent recession had hurt the shopkeepers and most, if not all of them, were unable to make payments on their loans, loans which he owned since he owned the bank as well. He had to give her credit though. Not many people had figured out that he was the owner of that particular bank. It wasn't as if he kept it a secret, but it wasn't advertised either.

She herself owned the ten-room inn and, although she'd kept up with her loan payments, he read between the lines and knew that she was having a hard time as well. He flipped to the next page and, sure enough, a report on her financials was right there. Hasif was thorough. Dassar once again had to give his chief advisor credit for knowing all of the details Dassar would require for his plan to work.

He flipped through some other pages, reading about her volunteer work, the animals she kept as pets and even the herbs she grew in her garden which were used in the recipes she baked for her small bed and breakfast inn. The woman was creative and had grown her business over the years. Unfortunately, she'd extensively renovated and expanded her inn's kitchen right before the recession hit. Although the economy was coming back and guests were starting to patronize her business once again, they weren't coming back fast enough for her to keep up with the hefty payment schedule.

She was beautiful, he thought, his thumb rubbing along the picture as if it were actually her skin.

But not for him, he thought and snapped the file closed. Looking up at the men waiting expectantly at the conference room table, he nodded, pretending that he hadn't just completely lost the thread of the conversation while reading through a profile on a stunningly beautiful woman. Clearing his head of the crazy idea of making such a soft, lovely and gentle woman his bride, he abruptly said, "Send me the list and we'll break down the top five." With that, he walked out of the conference room, holding onto both the file as well as the list of priorities for the revenues discussed in that meeting.

"Set up a meeting," he told Hasif, tucking the file underneath his arm. That statement in itself was surprising since he'd just rejected the idea because the woman seemed too soft and delicate. But his next words shocked even himself. "We'll fly out this weekend to finalize the issue. Ensure that extra guards are brought up to my training standards so that she has adequate protection after the wedding."

With that, Dassar moved on to the next issue on his day's agenda, once again pushing the issue of his impending nuptials out of his mind.

He was oblivious to the glee that briefly shone on his chief advisor's normally bland features with the dramatic decision.

Hasif moved off in the opposite direction, eager to tell the palace staff to pack up Faris' belongings. He was going to tell her as soon as he could find her that the sheik no longer had need of her services.

Chapter 2

"It isn't going to work," Barry said, handing her a bag of chicken feed.

"Of course it's going to work," Luna replied, accepting the bag and lugging it over her shoulder out of the shed. "The man isn't going to shut down the entire town."

"No, but he's probably going to sell off the assets so he can recoup his money." Barry walked behind her, wishing the Lovely Luna, as he referred to her in his mind, would let him do the heavy lifting for her. She was too slender, too slight of build to be lugging around those forty-pound bags of chicken feed.

Barry watched, unaware of the devotion that was shining through his eyes as he watched Luna spread the chicken feed out across the yard. She was sweet and wonderful and if she would only come out to dinner with him, he was sure he could prove to her that they could make it work.

"The whole town is gathering tonight to discuss the issue. It just doesn't make sense that he would evict an entire town, Barry." Luna bit her lip, hoping that her thinking was on target. She'd argued with everyone at last month's town meeting, telling them to at least give her plan a chance. Now she just had to prove that there was good in the world. She had to prove that this sheik guy was more than just a leader of a war-torn country. She knew that, deep down inside, everyone had a heart. Sometimes, it was just buried too deeply for a person to recognize that heart. This town had shown her that. Every person around this small town had taken her in and given her shelter in one way or another when she'd arrived here nine years ago. Ms. Prescott helped her catch up on all the math she'd missed, Barry's father had helped her with her readings skills, which were severely lacking because…well, because she'd fallen far behind in school back in New York.

Even her place here at the inn was because of the two ladies who had basically adopted her, watched over her, helped her heal. She'd come to this town broken and every person around had helped her to heal. So she wasn't going to give in until she gave back to them a little of what they'd done for her. She'd lost hope when she'd heard that her mother was gone. They'd given her a home, food, clothing and, most of all, hope. Hope in the goodness of the world.

The bank manager had already rejected her request. But she'd gone above him, only to be turned down by the odiously rude bank director. Never one to give up, she'd discovered that some sheik guy from that crazy country that had been at war for the past ten years actually owned the bank. So she'd tried one more time. So far, she hadn't received a rejection, so Luna was hopeful that there might be good news soon. No news meant no rejection, so she wasn't giving up hope.

"I don't have time to worry about it today though. Tonight is soon enough. I have a full house over the next few days," she told him. Turning to smile at Barry, she poured the rest of the bag of feed into the container, which would keep the chickens out but make tomorrow's feeding a bit easier. "And I'll make sure to encourage everyone to make their way to your art studio. Okay? See?" she said as she locked the bin and headed towards the kitchens again. "Everything is going to work out. A full house, lots of baked goods to sell, great art in your windows and even Mary Ann has doubled her chocolate goods for the weekend. Even she's optimistic that it will all work out. So why are you worrying?"

Barry shook his head as he watched Luna take off her boots, placing them carefully by the kitchen doorway. "You're just not realistic about how business works, Luna. I mean, why would the guy give us another chance?'

Luna was trying very hard not to lose patience with Barry's doom and gloom attitude, but it was growing tiresome. The man really was a worry-wart. Things worked out. They always worked out! She was living proof that things worked out when goodness and kindness prevailed. "Why wouldn't he? He's a businessman, right?"

"That is correct," a deep voice said from the kitchen doorway.

Luna spun around, a smile of greeting on her face. Which immediately froze when she caught sight of the man. He wasn't so much as standing in her doorway as overwhelming that limited space with his enormous size! She'd never seen a man as large and muscular as this man. Or as overtly terrifying either!

"Oh wow!" she whispered, taking in the tall, gorgeous man with shoulders that stretched across the expanse of the doorway. He actually had to duck as he walked into the room so that his head wouldn't smack into the top. And those eyes! Goodness, she looked up into those eyes and felt her heart beat faster. They were dark and mysterious and something just shot right through her. She could lose herself in those eyes, she thought.

Something nudged her arm but she didn't think anything of it, too amazed at the male specimen walking closer to her. But when Barry nudged her harder, she swung around to glare at him. Barry, in turn, looked at her pointedly.

Guests! "Oh! Right!" she gasped and snapped back to attention. "Right. Welcome!" she gushed. "I'm Luna Montgomery and welcome to the Moonside Inn," she told him. "Do you have reservations?" She gasped, "Oh, no! I hope you have reservations because otherwise, I might have to..." she shook her head. "No. I'm sure that everyone won't show up. We'll figure something out."

"We have reservations," the man standing in front of her said smoothly.

Dassar looked down at the blond woman and thought she was even more lovely in person. He hadn't thought that reality could live up to that picture of her smiling into the sunshine, but he had been wrong. This woman with her bright, blue eyes and platinum hair, she was simply beautiful. Her cheeks were the perfect color of a pink rose, a color which was only enhanced when she realized she'd been staring at him.

"Yes. Right!" she said again, receiving yet another nudge from Barry. "Stop that," she whispered furiously and stepped out of Barry's range so he couldn't nudge her again. "Anyway," she said, smiling up at the man. He really was amazingly attractive. That thin nose didn't detract from his looks in any way, she thought. And his hard jawline only made him look tougher in some way. Not at all like a male model. In fact, those pretty boys couldn't even come close to this man's raw, masculine appeal. Yes, they could take lessons from this man on how to appear manly.

"Luna!"

Luna jumped and turned to glare at Barry once again. "What?" she hissed.

"Stop staring," he admonished openly, the jealousy he was feeling hard to hide. Even Barry knew that he couldn't compare to this behemoth in the masculinity department, so he was eager for his Lovely Luna to get down to business so that the man would get out of her kitchen.

"I wasn't…" she looked up at the man, then blushed as she noticed he was still standing there, waiting for her to greet him correctly. "Oh. Well, so I am," she said out loud. "Anyway, yes…right. You have reservations." She wiped her hands on her jeans, wishing she was wearing something prettier, nicer, to greet this man. Or at least shoes, she thought and padded in her socks. She'd taken her boots off by the kitchen doorway, not wanting to track mud through her nice, clean kitchen. "This way," she told him and tried to slip past him. But he was too big and she had to halt, her eyes glancing up at him once again. "I can't get by," she whispered, her pulse pounding in her chest as her knees started to wobble. And it was all this man's fault!

Dassar looked down at the lovely woman, amusement shining out of his eyes. She was delightful, he thought. So innocent and naïve. Every thought was right there in her eyes and those blushes gave away her emotions too easily. No, this was not a good idea, he told himself. So why was he shifting slightly, giving her room to move into the receiving area of the inn?

She hesitated because he hadn't moved enough. And he should be a gentleman and give her more space, but he wanted to feel her softness just once before he left. She smelled good, he realized as she squeezed by him in the close confines of the kitchen doorway. She smelled like fresh air and…lemons.

Luna tried very hard not to touch this man, but it was impossible not to feel the hard power under her fingers as she slipped by him, her hands automatically shifting out to balance herself as she moved past him. "If you'll follow me, I'll get…" she looked around, startled by the large group of men standing in her receiving area. They all wore serious expressions, all were dressed in dark suits, although none looked as perfectly tailored as the tall man's suit, but they all looked very…manly.

"Right, I'll just get everyone checked in. You're under one reservation?" she asked, not sure what was going on. She was getting a dangerous vibe and wasn't sure what to make of it. Normally she trusted her instincts even though they'd led her astray on some occasions.

But in this instance, with the tall, sexy man right behind her, she was too flustered to listen to her instincts. She was actually too flustered to hold the pen she tried to pick up, but she finally managed to wrap her fingers around the pen, only to realize that she needed to check everyone in through the computer on the front desk. Dropping the pen, she pressed several buttons. It took her a few painful moments because her fingers had suddenly turned into all thumbs and she'd double hit one key and completely missed the key she was aiming for. It was all terribly embarrassing since normally, she was quite efficient. It was only because the enormous man was crowding her, standing so closely behind her that she could actually feel the heat of his body through the sweatshirt she was wearing. And she had absolutely no idea how to politely ask him to move away.

She pulled up the information for this weekend's guest reservations. "Um…Mr. Smith?" she asked, looking up.

A short, chubby man with merry eyes and a ready smile stepped forward. "That would be all of us. I made the reservation under that name to protect our identities."

Luna blinked, not sure what to make of that statement. "Okay. Well, I can keep a secret," she told the man. "Did you want to…" she thought quickly. Then smiled. "I'm sorry, but this is a bit clandestine. Normally people who want to hide their identities are trying to…" she looked around, about to make a teasing joke about how people come to hotels under the name "Smith" in order to have affairs. But as she took in the stern, intimidating expressions on each of the men's faces, she thought better of it. "Never mind," she told the man. Pressing a few more buttons. "I just need a credit card to cover incidentals," she told him. "And you've booked all ten rooms, is that correct?"

"That's correct," the man said, handing her a credit card under the name John Smith.

Luna looked at the card, immediately becoming suspicious. But she rang the card through and, sure enough, it came up as clear. Since all of the rooms had been paid for in advance, she wasn't sure what to say. "Okay then, here are the keys," she said, looking around. "Do you know who will be staying in each of the rooms?"

"We'll sort it out," he said. "Which is the best room?" he asked.

Luna blinked, berating herself for not pointing that out before she'd handed the man all of the keys. Her only excuse was that she was too flustered with the gorgeous guy behind her. She could feel his eyes on her, suspected that he knew she was wearing her Bugs Bunny underwear and wished she'd worn her black lace. But those things itched and Bugs was more fun.

Ugh! Concentrate, she told herself.

Her fingers shook as she pulled the appropriate key out of the stack. "This is the King's room," she explained. "It has a beautiful four poster bed, a fireplace and a separate sitting room. It's really lovely." She went on to explain the other rooms and their advantages and locations before the man bowed and stepped back.

"You have been very helpful."

She smiled gratefully. Breathing a sigh of relief that the check in process was finally over. "Dinner will be served starting at six o'clock across the street. There is a bar over to your left if you'd like drinks or coffee, tea, hot chocolate," she finished that one, feeling silly for saying that. These men definitely didn't drink hot chocolate. And she was pretty sure that none would enjoy the marshmallows that she kept on hand for anyone who really did like hot chocolate. She might be the only one in the room right now who would partake of that particular treat.

Taking a deep breath, she fought to keep her voice positive even though she'd very much like to duck under the front desk and wait until the big guy behind her had decided to move away and torment his next victim with his brooding x-ray vision. "Breakfast will be served tomorrow morning from seven until eleven and there are cookies and scones for an afternoon treat." She smiled brightly, feeling better now that she was on firmer territory. Who didn't like cookies and scones? Everyone loved them!

She brightened her smile, trying to appear professional and polite, despite her wobbly knees. "And if there is anything that you need, please don't hesitate to call me."

The men disappeared, some going upstairs swiftly, others moving towards the back of the inn and several more moved outside. She saw the outside men fan out and it looked suspiciously like they were looking for criminals. In her yard? The worst they might find was Dorothy, her lazy hound dog or Lucifer, the cat that came and went whenever he wanted food. This was a small town with only a few people living and working here. If one were to drive a couple of miles down the road, they would come to a bigger commercial area filled with all of the big box stores. But this town was small and they worked hard to keep it that way. There was an old-time feel to the shops that were enhanced by their location close to the various historical sites around the area.

It took less than three minutes for the room to clear out, but Luna knew that the man who had never been far from her mind was still behind her. Still staring at her butt. Darn it, she should have worn the black lace no matter how itchy they were.

"How long are you going to ignore me?" the man asked, amusement apparent in his deep voice.

Luna sighed and turned around, her hands clutching the front desk behind her for support. "I'm sorry. I wasn't trying to be rude. It's just that…" she wasn't sure what to say. "You are the sexiest thing that has ever crossed my path" just didn't seem like such a sophisticated thing to utter. This man looked like he ate monsters for breakfast, he was just that tough looking.

"Have a drink with me," he commanded and took her hand, leading her into the small sitting room. At one end of the room was a wooden bar, but it was closed since it was only eleven o'clock in the morning. But there was a coffee and tea service sitting out and she walked over to it, pouring him a cup of coffee. "How do you take it?" she asked, setting the delicate cup and saucer down on the tray table because the cup was clattering from her nervousness.

"You're nervous," he said and took the coffee urn, pouring her a cup and handing it to her. "Why?" he asked when they were both sitting down.

Luna didn't have the heart to tell him that she didn't drink coffee. She'd always found the taste too harsh. Bitter almost. So she set the cup on the small table beside her chair and rested her hands in her lap. "I'm sorry," she replied. "I don't know why I'm so nervous. It isn't like I haven't had men in the house before," she said, then stopped, looking across the small expanse at him, shocked at what she'd just said. "I mean…of course I haven't *been* with a man in the house…" her eyes closed and she shook her head. "I mean…" she wasn't sure what she meant any longer and when his laughter hit her, she just stopped talking.

When his laughter died down, he looked at her with amusement still shining through his dark eyes. "I suspect that I know what you mean, but I'm glad to hear that you don't normally carry on with men who stay at this beautiful inn. There must be ample opportunities for you to socialize though."

Luna breathed a sigh of relief, glad that he was letting her off the hook even though she was flubbing her lame attempt at sophisticated conversation. She simply wasn't a sophisticated kind of woman. She was just down to earth, what-you-see-is-what-you-get type of person. "No. Not really. The inn takes up a great deal of my time."

Dassar couldn't believe that this woman, with her silver hair and her bright, eager eyes with the slanting, cat-like glance, hadn't been propositioned by numerous men over the years. She was too beautiful, too enticing. "But the other guests who come to stay overnight, surely some have been interested."

She shook her head. "No. This is an out of the way location. Anyone coming here is staying for a romantic getaway with their significant other," she smiled. "So the men are mostly taken."

"Good to know. And what about your boyfriend?" he asked, probing mercilessly but unconcerned with how he was perceived. This was to be his wife, his queen and he wanted to know more about her. Everything was telling him that she wouldn't work out, that he should turn and walk away. He needed a woman who could be strong under pressure, who would be able to handle herself with him. He knew that he wasn't the easiest man to live with. But his wife would have to be faithful.

Luna shook her head. "I'm not seeing anyone," she said but not sure why she was admitting all of this to this stranger. She suddenly realized that she didn't even know his name. How could she have revealed so much to a stranger? But for some reason, he didn't feel like a stranger. As she looked into his dark eyes, she sensed that this tall, intimidating man was just as lonely in his high-pressure occupation as she was despite both of them being surrounded by people almost constantly.

How crazy was that, she thought? A man as gorgeous and sexy as this man couldn't possibly be lonely. But still....

"What about the man in the kitchen? The one who kept punching you."

Luna laughed, the idea of her and Barry as a couple was ludicrous. "Barry? Oh goodness, he's just a friend." She was watching the man under her lashes and thought she sensed a relaxing in his shoulders with her statement. But that was impossible.

"So you are the owner here," he stated with a change of subject. Dassar was satisfied that she was relatively innocent, although he suspected she wasn't a virgin. No woman who looked like she did and was as open and honest as she was could remain untouched. He didn't like it, but he definitely liked her. "Tell me what it is like to own a small inn like this?"

"Oh, the cleaning and early mornings are a bit of a problem for me, since I love sleeping in and I absolutely hate doing laundry." She smiled even as she crinkled up her nose at the confession. "But I love cooking, which compensates for the rest of the chores. Just wait until you try my scones. They're really amazing," she told him.

"I will anticipate that experience with relish," he replied. He was truly enchanted by her enthusiasm, but hated the idea of this woman cleaning. Looking down, he realized that her hands were red, obviously used to the harsh chemicals needed to freshen up a hotel room after guests had stayed overnight. He'd have to speak to Hasif about getting her some help. He didn't like the idea of this little woman with her soft, beautiful skin, having to clean up after guests.

No, he couldn't marry this woman, but he could definitely make her life easier, he thought.

He stood up, determined to find Hasif and tell him they could leave. "Perhaps you would be kind enough to have dinner with me tonight?" Those words surprised even him, but the look on the lovely woman's face told him that she was surprised as well.

Luna stood as well, preferring not to look up at him quite so much. But the man was so tall that even standing still caused her to have to tilt her head back. "I'm so sorry," she gushed sincerely. "But I already have a big meeting with some people tonight and I can't miss it."

Dassar bowed slightly. "Another time then," and he walked out of the room. She was wrong for him, he thought again as he ascended the stairs. But she was beautiful and she stirred something inside of him that he hadn't felt in a long time. Actually, never, he realized. There was lust, absolutely, but there was something more, something that he couldn't quite define because he wasn't familiar with the sensation.

Surely it wasn't protectiveness, he thought. No, that was ridiculous.

He went upstairs and spoke to Hasif about other matters, the issue of the lovely Luna spinning around in his mind. In the end, he shook his head.

"I can't marry the woman," he told his chief advisor.

Hasif had recognized the signs in this man. He was interested in the woman. More than interested. And from the small bit of interaction he'd witnessed, Luna Montgomery was exactly what this man, and Altair, needed. She would bring life and happiness to this man. She was filled with hope and optimism. She was perfect.

But he had to be careful.

"Perhaps you are right," he said and started gathering up the papers he and Dassar had been working on moments ago. "Another man might be better suited to marry her."

Hasif wasn't looking, but he could feel the rise in tension. After only a few minutes in the woman's company, Dassar was smitten. And his ruler certainly wouldn't like the idea of another man touching what Hasif suspected Dassar already considered his woman. Moments later, his suspicions were confirmed.

"This is a good place to relax and get some of the issues worked out," he announced. "So we will stay here for a few days and work on the details of that construction plan and the military bases."

Hasif didn't even crack a smile. He simply gathered up the papers and bowed out of the room. "Yes, Your Highness."

List of Elizabeth Lennox Books

The Texas Tycoon's Temptation

The Royal Cordova Trilogy
Escaping a Royal Wedding
The Man's Outrageous Demands
Mistress to the Prince

The Attracelli Family Series
Never Dare a Tycoon
Falling For the Boss
Risky Negotiations
Proposal to Love
Love's Not Terrifying
Romantic Acquisition

The Billionaire's Terms: Prison or Passion
The Sheik's Love Child
The Sheik's Unfinished Business
The Greek Tycoon's Lover
The Sheik's Sensuous Trap
The Greek's Baby Bargain
The Italian's Bedroom Deal
The Billionaire's Gamble
The Tycoon's Seduction Plan
The Sheik's Rebellious Mistress
The Sheik's Missing Bride
Blackmailed by the Billionaire
The Billionaire's Runaway Bride
The Billionaire's Elusive Lover
The Intimate, Intricate Rescue

The Sisterhood Trilogy
The Sheik's Virgin Lover
The Billionaire's Impulsive Lover
The Russian's Tender Lover
The Billionaire's Gentle Rescue

The Tycoon's Toddler Surprise
The Tycoon's Tender Triumph

The Friends Forever Series
The Sheik's Mysterious Mistress
The Duke's Willful Wife
The Tycoon's Marriage Exchange

The Sheik's Secret Twins
The Russian's Furious Fiancée
The Tycoon's Misunderstood Bride

Love By Accident Series
The Sheik's Pregnant Lover
The Sheik's Furious Bride
The Duke's Runaway Princess

The Russian's Pregnant Mistress

The Lovers Exchange Series
The Earl's Outrageous Lover
The Tycoon's Resistant Lover

The Sheik's Reluctant Lover
The Spanish Tycoon's Temptress

The Berutelli Escape
Resisting The Tycoon's Seduction
The Billionaire's Secretive Enchantress

The Big Apple Brotherhood
The Billionaire's Pregnant Lover
The Sheik's Rediscovered Lover

The Tycoon's Defiant Southern Belle

The Sheik's Dangerous Lover (Novella)

The Thorpe Brothers
His Captive Lover
His Unexpected Lover
His Secretive Lover
His Challenging Lover

The Sheik's Defiant Fiancée (Novella)
The Prince's Resistant Lover (Novella)
The Tycoon's Make-Believe Fiancée (Novella)

The Friendship Series
The Billionaire's Masquerade
The Russian's Dangerous Game
The Sheik's Beautiful Intruder

The Love and Danger Series – Romantic Mysteries
Intimate Desires
Intimate Caresses
Intimate Secrets
Intimate Whispers

The Alfieri Saga
The Italian's Passionate Return (Novella)
Her Gentle Capture
His Reluctant Lover
Her Unexpected Admirer
Her Tender Tyrant
Releasing the Billionaire's Passion (Novella)
His Expectant Lover

The Sheik's Intimate Proposition (Novella)

The Hart Sisters Trilogy
The Billionaire's Secret Marriage
The Italian's Twin Surprise (USA Today™ Best Seller!)
The Forbidden Russian Lover (USA Today™ Best Seller!)

The War, Love, and Harmony Series
Fighting with the Infuriating Prince (Novella)
Dancing with the Dangerous Prince (Novella)
The Sheik's Secret Bride
The Sheik's Angry Bride
The Sheik's Blackmailed Bride
The Sheik's Convenient Bride

The Boarding School Series – September 2015 to January 2016
The Boarding School Series Introduction
The Greek's Forgotten Wife
The Duke's Blackmailed Bride
The Russian's Runaway Bride
The Sheik's Baby Surprise
The Tycoon's Captured Heart

www.ingramcontent.com/pod-product-compliance
Lightning Source LLC
Chambersburg PA
CBHW060647130626
46555CB00002B/989